this is
how it
took
place

this is how it took place

Rudrakshi Bhattacharjee

Selected and Edited by Shinie Antony

HarperCollins *Publishers* India

First published in India by
HarperCollins *Publishers* in 2019
A-75, Sector 57, Noida, Uttar Pradesh 201301, India
www.harpercollins.co.in

2 4 6 8 10 9 7 5 3 1

'This Is How It Took Place' first published in *The Adroit Journal*
'La Mer' first published in *So to Speak*

P-ISBN: 978-93-5357-383-6
E-ISBN: 978-93-5357-384-3

Typeset in 11/15 Garamond at
Manipal Digital Systems, Manipal

Printed and bound at
Thomson Press (India) Ltd

FSC
MIX
Paper
FSC® C010615

For Sammy
and all those who seek to see beyond

CONTENTS

BA 777 TO ATHENS IS DELAYED

It seems as if I have been waiting here for years.

The bright lights, the steel monochrome, the mechanized smell dull my senses and I find my eyes closing of their own volition. When I arrived at the airport three hours ago, I did not think my flight to Athens would be delayed by twelve hours. So now I am here, resting on these flat black seats with ivory handles that obstruct my body from finding a comfortable position.

A person passes by every ten minutes or so and the smell of coffee from the cup they inevitably carry jolts me awake. An elderly man walks by and I stare at him, at the tufts of white hair sprinkled on his round head and chin. He seems tired, more than what is caused by a delayed flight; his head is drooping and the wiry smile on his face seems a little too crooked. He does not appear to have any luggage, and when he sits down a few seats from me, staring straight ahead with unblinking, steely-grey eyes, I imagine his wife has left him and he is now going to find her and bring her back. It's a wistful idea, the remnants of a childhood dream of endless true love.

The next person to pass by is a thin, pale woman with her shoulders hunched and her mouth pursed into a tight 'o'. Her hand is on her son's back and her fingers are coiled around him tightly, as if someone might try to take him away any moment.

This time it's not the smell of an espresso that awakens me but the sweet smell of candy. The boy has opened a packet of gummy bears and he gnaws through it ferociously, and I almost laugh because he is holding his candy with the same protectiveness his mother holds him.

No one appears for another twenty minutes and I busy myself with a nearby *Health* magazine, listening intently to the robotic voice that rings through every few minutes with information about different flights. It is almost god-like how the woman reciting the timings has my fate in her hands and she doesn't even know it.

A couple appears, laughing and exchanging glances, disrupting the sombre mood of the waiting area. They settle down on the seats with a loud thud and the woman with the son scoffs. Bitterness, I think, wafts through all of us, ready to be incited by almost anything.

The couple's chatter picks up to a torrential pace and I cannot make out what they are saying in an unfamiliar language, but their voices together sound like the crinkling of gift-wrapping paper. I try to remember the last time I was as happy.

I look over at the woman with the son and see that the boy is now picking out his last gummy bear. I watch his solemn face as he slowly nibbles on the edge of the neon-pink gummy bear before the temptation gets too much for him and he pops it into his mouth. Then he pulls at his mother's shirt, rubbing her arms and pleading for more, and I think of going up to him and offering to buy it for him.

I look over at the escalator to my left and am surprised by the sheer number of people who are walking up and down. So many people, so many lives I know nothing about.

I look over at the boy again and something about the cross look on his face and the scratchy quality of his voice almost draws me to him. But this is not the time, nor the place.

The waiting area around me which seemed so empty hours ago is now brimming with people. There are bodies sprawled all over the black seats and there are so many faces that it feels impossible to try to recall even one. We are to each other a faceless, nameless crowd conjoined by a common purpose. Just then, it seems disappointing that all we will remember of each other is one delayed flight.

THIS IS HOW IT TOOK PLACE

This is how I remember Antony: sentient and aberrant. Curved chin, topaz jaw, hair sprouting out of his bottle-shaped head. Not beautiful, never that, but intriguing. Rising from beneath the water, his arms on mine, the veins in his neck bulging like thin green snakes trying to push their way out of his skin. Laughing sometimes, throat quivering, chapped lips and a mouth suddenly penetrable. His laugh has always been a quiet, rustling sound; you can hear it only if you try. Then he is beneath the water again, absolved, as if he was never there at all.

I don't remember how I started cheating on Mark with Antony, but I remember it happened very fast. I knew Antony's apartment address in a day, his allergies (pollen and tobacco sauce) in another, his relationship with his parents (non-existent) in a week. Somehow my life formed a routine. I spent my days with Mark and my nights with Antony. Comedy shows and then Godard films. Discussions about Central Park and then the Met. Loud, buzzing groups with mimosas and then a solemn bottle of wine. Sometimes I liked to pretend they were

9

the same person and that he was just different in the morning
and in the evening. Two sides to the same person. I'll never get
bored, I told myself. It's like the perfect partner. A two-in-one
deal. I repeated this to myself continuously – in cabs, on the
subway, standing on pavements as I stared at the reflection of
my face in rain puddles, wondering when I had started looking
as drained as a rotten grape. They were very similar though,
and this made it easier to pretend. Mark liked his coffee with
no sugar, as did Antony. Both loved the idea of winter, but
admitted that a hot summer was easier to bear. They had
both been on their respective school swimming teams. Both
worked in sales, although one was a cashier, the other a regional
manager. They could have almost been best friends. Meeting
on the C train, drinking chilled beers after work, kicking back
their feet and loosening their collar and discussing women and
sports. I like to think of them that way: old friends fitting into
each other comfortably, always laughing at a joke I had told.

An example of a conversation with Antony: 'We spent our
nights on the streets, just walking and looking at the guys selling
their paintings. It was beautiful in a way I don't think I'll ever
experience again.' Antony pulled at my earlobes the way Mark
pulled at my toes. 'Did you ever buy a painting?' Antony sighed,
smoke blew into my face. 'We were broke and in college. English
majors. We still can't afford paintings.'

'You're not a failure. And you can now.'

'It's almost as if you think I love you because you flatter me.'

'You were young and dumb then – I'm sure you bought
some obscure painting. Half a breast, face of a lion.'

'We were young.'

We were young. Antony said this often, and only when I had not met him for a few days. It was a sore point with him. That he was forty-five and I was twenty-seven and Mark twenty-eight. I told him it's scandalous. I told him age looks good on him. I told him I'll love him when he's grey. I told him all the things I was supposed to tell him. His eyes gleamed, his fingers jokingly reaching for an aspirin lying on the table because he knew that I knew that later he would rummage for Benzedrine in his bathroom cupboards. I wish I could describe the pathos that Antony's tired figure evinced from me anytime I touched his pulsing warm body as he talked in a flurry of drunken murmurs, even though he had not touched a drop of alcohol. Antony's guzzling brown irises dilated, the whites of his eyes disappearing. I was always rapacious about Antony's eyes, I imagined myself swallowing them while I lay with Mark.

On an afternoon I spent with Laura in a Fifth Avenue restaurant I could barely afford, she called Antony the Mysterious Musician even though I had told her numerous times that Antony had never played a musical instrument. 'That doesn't matter,' she had said, 'he just has to be the type.' I told her she had been watching too many romantic comedies. Laura didn't find the age thing as strange as I thought she would. But then again, her husband was six years younger than her; she couldn't judge. Laura met Antony once. She said he was gruff and smug and she made me wonder when I had stopped seeing him the way everyone else saw him. We argued.

'But Mark's so much better for you. He's so nice.'

'I think so too.'

'Then why not drop Antony?' She cupped my face. She thought I liked it when she treated me like her daughter, she thought I had never been shown affection without lust accompanying it. All this analysis from a psych class she had taken in community college more than three decades ago. I called her Grizzly Bear in my head, and not only because she never shaved properly so she pricked my skin anytime her legs brushed against mine. 'And stay with Mark. I understand the need to break out and try a dangerous thing, but it has been a year now. I mean I get it, the literature thing. But he has the personality of a brush.'

'I'm just enjoying myself.'

She petted me disconcertedly before licking the large brownie on her plate and gulping it down. As I stared at the thin wrinkles on her face that made it look like she was always squinting and the alarming whiteness of her hair, I wondered why I continually surrounded myself with people who were at least ten years older than me.

'Just don't get too attached. What happens if Mark doesn't forgive you?'

I didn't see her much after that.

Places I have visited with Mark:

A deli on a street in Chelsea that we found by accident

Coney Island

A YouTube Space Gordo's Bar
An open mic night at an LGBTQ friendly bar where Mark sang *'My heart will go on'*
The Strand
Mark's parents' house on the Upper East Side
Staten Island.

Places I have visited with Antony:
His apartment.

When I first told Mark I loved him, it was because of how he smelled that day. He smelled like detergent and smoked ham. He reminded me of the liveliness of a Sunday brunch and the openness of cafés with rooftop seating. He reminded me of houses with long hallways and mirrors running from one end to the other. He reminded me of baby-blue walls and bright orange curtains and white fruit bowls and marble kitchen islands. When I first told Mark I loved him, he bought me a gold pendant. When we fought, I gave it back. When we made up, he gave me a new one. This was how it was with Mark. Endless chances and charity donations. A life of two kids, country clubs and a tennis court on which he would let me win if I asked.

Antony, I knew, I would never marry. It wasn't even because we rarely agreed or because there were always aching silences between us or because he was always so angry that he needed to chew Benzedrine to sit upright. It wasn't even because anytime I kissed him I had to pretend I could not taste the sour bite of a previous cigarette or because I never knew what he was going to do until he did it. It wasn't even the age thing, although I had wondered about that at first. It was because when I told him I was with Mark, he scowled and then laughed and said, 'I'm sorry that this has happened. And I'm sorry that I love you as well.'

Towards the end of my relationship with Antony and the start of my marriage with Mark, Antony finally began to share his poems with me. He was like a more callous Allen Ginsberg and sometimes I found him dry and witless. But I liked the idea of having my very own Beat poet, tightened and caged and leashed to me. I only seemed to live for the idea of things, I was slowly realizing. I never had any time to give to the reality of situations.

The reason I broke up with Antony and spent three weeks in misery while Mark rubbed my back, applied ointment and combed my hair before finally proposing to me was because of what Antony said when I told him I didn't want to choose between him and Mark. He said, 'And that's another thing I hate about women. A woman finds a million ways to tell a man he's useless without having to say it out loud.' I told him I always knew he hated women. He chuckled. It was a *really* ugly, throaty sound. I only thought it was a chuckle because it was easier to think that than think of it as something harsher, like the clearing of his throat. 'Even my barber knows that.'

I told him he was a homosexual. Then I told him I didn't mind if he was, but that I'd known all along. 'I'm not gay,' he said. 'I've let you into my house for so long, haven't I?' I asked him why he was so angry about Mark. He'd never said anything before. Why was he asking about Mark now? 'Because I didn't realize I could until today.'

Then I left his apartment, not even turning around once. Within three months, I was back. It was eleven, I took a cab even though the fare came to sixty dollars, but with my new name and bank account of Mrs Mark, I had been promised that money did not matter. We would have to save, yes, but not in the way I had been saving when I lived in Brooklyn. 'You can withdraw and withdraw,' Mark had said to me in the way you tell a child he can have as many red toy trucks as he wants. 'Anything you need.' Mark smiled, and his teeth suddenly seemed too white to me, as if he'd had them removed and replaced with a shinier ivory set he thought would look much better.

Antony scowled at me the entire time I talked. The hollows of his cheeks gaped at me, the dark circles around his eyes glowered. I wanted to touch his face and feel its bristly edges. I wanted to kiss him right above his chin where he had cut himself shaving. I wanted to scream at him that it wasn't fair that the reasons I had fallen in love with him were the reasons I couldn't stay. He said: 'I did miss you.' I said, 'I was in Paris. Love and all that.' He said, 'My subscription to the *Leopard's Review* got over.' I said, 'I'll buy you a new one.' He said, 'Buy me a new fridge too while you're at it.'

Sometimes I would think about poisoning Mark while I sat at my desk in the library, doing no justice to the managerial position he had got for me. I thought of slipping some antifreeze in the cranberry juice I would give him while we'd sit on our terrace, looking at the building opposite where he wanted to live because it had bigger rooms and a bigger terrace and more floors. I would love him then, I decided, I would be so kind to him that day. I would grin at every joke he cracked, I would rub his back, I would do all the things he had done for me. I would feel sad, maybe even cry a little once he was dead, but the thrill of taking away his life, of being so powerful, lit a sort of burning desire in me. My body suddenly felt alive and jocular; it was like I had been reminded that my body was my own and my life was my own and I could do whatever I wanted. It seemed like a tremendous finding to me, this simple thought that I could do what I wanted, that tomorrow I could run away to Bali or throw myself off a cliff because my life was mine. I had forgotten I had a pulse for so long that now, when it became apparent to me once again, I felt it with such a deep and powerful throbbing that it seemed impossible to ignore. It became more and more clear to me that I could only love Mark if I was going to leave him.

This is the way in which Antony becomes angry:

First, he will shake his head slightly and scoff, releasing a sudden whoosh of air from his mouth. Then he will sit down on whatever is near him, be it a table, a chair; at times even the floor will do. Then he will stare at me, threatening me to continue. I will continue. Then he will look down and close his eyes, and I will imagine that when he opens his eyes again, they will glow a violent shade of red and he will sprout out fingers like Edward Scissorhands and slice me into thin, creamy pieces of flesh so he can keep me cooped up in some jar he has forgotten to clean in his kitchen. But he will not do any of this.

Instead he will laugh and take me into his arms, and I will apologize and he will say, 'You do like me, don't you?' and I will say, 'Not always, not now, maybe yesterday,' and he will smile because he finds me funny and I will stay there sprawled out on his chest, chin up, watching his rubbery purple lips murmur something in Latin, and I will say, 'Why did you learn a dead language?' and he will say, 'To impress you,' and I will not say anything because now in this moment we are in a movie, in a romantic comedy, and I can feel nothing except this sort of bubbling happiness, because to love and to know that you are loved is enough, it's enough for me, and we will stay like this till Antony's skin withers away and flakes of his dead skin fall to the floor, and I will stay there buried in his skeleton until that too breaks and I am left with only this memory of him and then I will mourn, mourn, mourn.

This is the way in which Antony tells me he's leaving:

'I'm going back to Kansas.' He's eating the maple-sugar-and-honey oats I bought him from CVS, and is picking out the dried raisins because he thinks they look like dead insects. 'My mother's dead.'

'I thought you lived in Missouri.'

'Kansas City,' he growls. 'Anyway, I'm leaving soon, my brother wants me there for the funeral to say a few words. And

I haven't seen my nephew in a while, so I've bought a bike for him. This is pretty much my last day with you. I'll be home for a while.'

I watch him. He looks as haggard as always with his ruffled hair and his untucked shirt and his blue Under Armour boxers which he has worn every time I've met him. But there's something different, something so out of place it's disconcerting. He's grinning. His face looks like those lopsided colourful smiley faces children make with play dough. He looks like Mark.

'I'm sorry,' he says. 'I'm sorry to put you through all this. Don't forget me.'

'How can I forget a poet as famous as you?' I say and I am supposed to sound bitter but I just sound pathetic. Like I'm begging him to stay.

He laughs. It is settled.

When I get back home to Mark, I tell him that I had been having an affair for the entirety of our relationship. I tell Mark about Antony's retarded brother, his alcoholic sister, his dead mother, his broken cobblestone home, his favourite yoghurt shop where he was kissed by a senior girl and the park nearby where his friend was shot. Then I cry because I am getting mixed up, because Antony's brother might have been a construction worker, he may not have a sister, he might have lived on a farm and his friend might as well be alive and well and working with Goldman Sachs. I can believe anything I want because I will never know the truth again.

'Why did you marry me?' Mark says. He is making a sandwich with only lettuce and chunky pieces of cream cheese between the bread.

'I love you,' I say. It's like another way of saying sorry. 'I love you.'

'Why did you marry me?' he says again and takes out taco shells from the cupboard. Mark once told me he loves Mexican food because the best days of his life were the holidays he spent with his aunt in Tijuana. He helped her sew when she couldn't any more because of her arthritis and in return she would give him cochinita pibil, which he would give the boys near his aunt's house so that they would agree to play soccer with him. When he had told me this, I suggested we go to Chipotle.

'I am not particularly rich, or handsome, or clever. Why did you marry me?'

Mark does not get angry in the way Antony gets angry. When Mark gets angry, he bites his nails or peels off his scabs or cooks sporadically. When Mark gets angry he does not shout; he discusses.

'Ow!' he yelps suddenly; his fingers have brushed the pan in which he is making tomato sauce. His iPhone beeps and he flinches in surprise.

I cannot think of a life without him.

Weeks later, Antony emails me pictures of himself with his family. He looks like a child in all of them. He is eating corndogs and making silly faces with his sister. I email him back and ask him if he has found a writing job there yet. He tells me his brother got him a job in construction. *Your mother is dead*, I want to remind his smiling face. But I don't say anything and I delete his contact from my phone.

When Mark asks me why I did it, why I hurt him like I did, I am not sure how to respond. He looks at me expectantly, waits for me to say something like I have so much love that I can't contain it, but I disappoint him. I say, 'I'm sorry,' and he says, 'I know you are but what am I,' and he laughs, but he rarely comes home now. He spends all his time in his office or at the gym. Sometimes I go through his phone when he is in the shower, quickly skimming through his messages. So far I am safe – Mark only texts his friends things like account numbers and questions about holidays; there are no women. There is one other text he sends every Friday, where he asks, 'How much?' and the response comes, '$250 for an ounce of MJ,' and Mark says, 'Meet at the location,' but I don't mind. Mark and I are happy.

MY GRANDMOTHER SAW HER REFLECTION AND
COULDN'T HELP BUT WALK INTO IT

When I went to call my grandmother, expecting her to cackle and offer me green-tea gum, I did not expect to see how she had shattered her body in the night.

Her head lay bashed in, pieces of glass piercing through her hair, which used to be the colour of nougat but was now sprinkled with what looked like strawberry jam. The mirror, which used to stand in front of her, now contorted her face; it upturned her mouth into a long grin, a final sizzle, a last offering.

When I told Uncle what she had done, his cheeks beamed cherry red. Crumbs of the cupcake Grandmother had baked hung to his ruffled beard and fell into my mouth when he came close and boxed both my ears as he asked why I had pushed her into the glass.

I lay down next to my grandmother and snuggled into her chest as I waited for her to laugh and tell me the joke she had said she would when I had gone to call on her last Friday afternoon.

WALKING WITH MY FRIENDS TO THE BUS STOP

I am walking with my friends and we are on the rough brown pavement that leads away from school towards the yellow fleeing buses which glint like far-off jewels in the bristling afternoon light.

Without even realizing it, I fall behind, and now the sounds my friends make are no longer sweet and guileless like the crinkling of wrapping paper on one of our birthdays or the popping of bubble sheets on lazy Sunday afternoons. The sounds turn slow and menacing, erupting from my friends' throats with the deftness of a hiss from a cornered snake or a low growl from a dog left with its last piece of meat.

My friends change their positions swiftly, moving from one companion to the next, each not left alone for more than a moment, words upon words upon words, sentences blubbered out quickly, and I marvel at my friends' ability to speak without saying anything at all.

Their movement is like the shifting of the tectonic plates that lie under our feet, in constant motion, and it seems like nothing is going to change and then you step back and realize you are not where you once were and you are not where you once thought you'd be and you are not with the people you promised yourself you would remember in ten years.

Sometimes I am able to catch up with my friends and their limp arms bump into mine and I can smell the vanilla perfume we had bought together on our first trip to the mall without our parents and I am reminded of the wholesomeness of the familiarity one gains from having spent an entire life together, from having walked to the bus stop together every day.

But then I trip, and my friends are moving away too fast for me to reach them and I am so far behind them that I only see the ends of their dusty sports shoes and their legs which look like peach ladles. They are bounding away and crushing the spines of fallen leaves, breaking the bones of venturing scorpions, leaping into the oncoming dusk.

My friends are not mindful; they pretend not to hear the gravel croak under their weight, they pretend not to hear me scream each time their hurried, heavy voices chorus in laughter as I stumble forward, as I miss a step.

Soon their words slip into a garbled tongue which I cannot unmask and now, in spite of it all, I am running behind them, and it is years from now and my friends are smiling at me from behind their ivory towers, their silver skyscrapers, and my arms are flailing after them pitifully, and I am choking on the fumes from the exhaust of the buses and I am struggling to catch up. As I am coughing and spluttering, I can only think of what a mess we have made, of what terrible things my friends and I have done, of the trees that are yet to be trampled upon, of the mute hills still not dug, of the azure sky that we will one day set alight.

Every day it is becoming more and more difficult to make the simple trip to the bus stop with my friends by my side.

WHO ELSE WILL LOVE THE DAMNED?

When I went to visit my sister in the hospital against my mother's orders, I wondered if I should've just stayed home instead. It was a Friday, but a curious one, because it was the first Friday I had ever skipped school in almost two years. My parents were ruthless when it came to taking a break, or ever just staying home because *I* was tired, because *I* wanted just one day off. God forbid I ever made the mistake of deliberately missing the bus, or loafing around in the morning. My parents would make sure that I would never want to miss a day of school again. My mother would snipe at me throughout the day, every comment traced with some sort of vicious backhanded afterthought. *I thought you still had some sort of ambition left in you,* is what she said to me once, in a sudden hiss born of her surly breath. *I actually thought you wouldn't waste your life, wouldn't waste your time.* At other times, what she said was more repugnant simply because it was true. And because my mother had an uncanny ability to sense where the blade would draw the most blood when she struck it. *Another plate, really, this is the age when you start to gain, don't be naive, you know how fast you put on.* Her slippery tongue sliding in like a snake's. Still, my mother's attacks came in the form of prickly murmurs and assaults, her missiles designed only to make her dumb second daughter more introspective and aware. Her words were like sharp pinpricks: they hit the spot but didn't stay buried too long. My mother, although she was brittle and angry and malicious, did not find pleasure in hurting me. I understand now, I suppose, that all my mother was trying to do was make sure that I would not turn into my sister.

My father, on the other hand, would deliver his words in the form of bombs and grenades. Where my mother was precise, my father was more tumultuous and haphazard; shouting and bellowing, his eyes widening into the shape of full, ripe plums, a most violent shade of red. Not to say that my father's shaky yet forceful words didn't have an impact on me. In fact, I can remember the countless nights I spent crying in bed, sobbing into my pillow to muffle the sound. That is something I still take pride in: whatever happened, I never let my parents see me cry. It was the only sort of defence I could muster against the tireless trials my parents put me through because I had no arms against them. I was not frightfully clever, and could not (although I tried several times) come up with an ingenious plan that would get them to pay for their words. Instead, I just created a distinct atmosphere of coolness between my parents and me – I did not join them when they talked in the evenings, I walked the other way if I saw them coming towards me, and I studied all hours of the day in the hope that they would leave me alone at mealtimes.

And there was my sister: sitting on the hospital bed, looking out of the white shuttered window, her hair shorter than a boy's, exposing her long, polished neck. Her green feline eyes were as shrewd as always, narrowed down at me, and I knew she was thinking several thoughts all at once. I felt the usual bitter resentment strike up within me again. Even ill, with her arms bandaged up in a thick, ugly plaster, and dressed in a horrible urine-yellow gown, she was lovely. Her slender arms, her thin, flat waist, her waifish figure. I wondered what I might have done had I possessed my sister's body, my sister's beauty. Would I have been as elusive as her, allowing everyone to wonder, to fashion some sort of persona for me in their own minds, relishing the sweetness of who I was because they did not know me? For I had figured out, in my fourteen years with my sister, that creating new personalities to greet someone with was what she loved to do. I might've done the same, had my face not had this grainy texture, had my body not had this dumpy shape.

'Are you better now?' It was a stupid question. A stupid question my sister would not answer.

'I won't do it again, if that's what you're asking. I thought Mom told you not to come.'

A gulp. 'I had to, you know that. I ... I mean ... I care about you, right?'

My sister would usually have her cigarette and lighter out by now.

'Ask me. Don't pretend. Ask me why I did it. You're obsessed with me anyway.' Up came her face, ghoulish, out came her voice, bedraggled.

As I stared at her arched body, her smooth limp fingers coiled around her toes, tearing out her long flaky toenails, leaving behind jagged edges of skin, I realized that my sister wanted me to go away so she could cry.

'I've seen you watch me with my friends, with him. It's sick, you know that. You probably hoped I was dead so you could take my place. God, you even tried to look through my phone once, I saw you.'

'Mom asked me to.'

'You fucking doormat.'

I wanted to slap my sister. Tear her ragged bandages off and slice up her skin. Bite her long, cream-coloured neck and thrash her. *What your sister needs,* my father had once said when my sister had screamed at him for hours, after she had taunted him endlessly, *is a really good beating.* When I thought about it, that was how my sister behaved with everyone. She snapped at them, she pushed them around smugly, biting at them with my mother's precision, my mother's grace, when she was in a good enough mood for conversation, when it had been a good enough day for her. But I had seen her on bad days. I had seen her explode, screaming incoherently, blazing through anyone who dared to talk to her. But I don't think it was ever contempt or condescension that my sister felt for the people around her. Although it certainly seemed like my sister was a boiling, furious person every time she fought with me, yelling insults at the top of her lungs or murmuring derision and spite, I knew my sister was not angry; nothing as buoyant as that. Now that I look back, what I mistook for vehemence in my sister's attacks, in her daily disdain, in her ever-accusing *there's something seriously wrong with you* was sheer hopelessness on her part. My sister felt for herself a hatred so great and overbearing that she could barely contain it. So her self-loathing spilled out of her cracking skin, falling away and attacking anyone around.

I felt sorry for my sister then. I felt sorry that my sister, despite her wit and her intelligence and her beauty, was always going to be alone. Alone with the fear that she was not nearly as enigmatic and perplexing as people thought her to be, alone with the fear that she would have to pretend, and pretend through the rest of her life, pretending for anyone she met.

'Are you going to be discharged?' I touched my sister's body, my sister's bruised and battered body, and rubbed her back slowly. I could smell her pungent sweat. I could feel the ends of her jaggedly cut hair.

'I don't know. I'll be in-patient for a while.'

'You'll stay here? Here?'

'I don't mind, really.'

When I got home, my mother looked like she'd been ravaged and stripped of her dignity. Her hair lay in shambles, she was wearing an overflowing, pink nightie and sucking on a long orange carrot, her teeth grinding against each other like gravel under a tyre.

'Where have you been?'

I told her.

'What is wrong with you? Do you have any regard for what is right?'

I told her I did, and that was why I went to see my sister.

37

'Do you understand that your sister is sick? Do you know what sick means?'

'She's not sick, Mom, just tired.'

'It means that she doesn't live in the same world as us. She's being pulled away by a tide that she cannot control. Something like that.'

She's just tired, Mom, I think she just wants to sleep, it's nothing as poetic as a tide she cannot control.

'Do you know what your sister did? Do you understand that it's wrong?'

I'm not blind, Mom, I saw the bandages, I saw the cuts. You can say it. My sister slit her wrists. My sister slit her wrists because she didn't have the courage to do anything else. It wasn't wrong, Mom. It was her decision.

'I hope you understand that that kind of thing is not tolerated in a family like ours.'

Yes, ma'am.

'I only want the best for you. I just want to carry on like normal.'

Yes, ma'am.

'You can skip school tomorrow, if you like. Just one day.'

No, ma'am.

ROMEO AND JULIET – I

What is life? No one really knows the answer. I don't mean the scientific explanation; I've got that memorized. No, I mean the answer from inside. I mean your original, uncorrupted, non-trying answer. That's what I want to know. That's all I'm looking for. I don't want money or fame, just the answer – the answer to the simplest question in the world. If the question is so easy, why isn't the answer? Even world-renowned geniuses would have a hard time answering this question.

Ever since I was a little girl, I've been trying to understand what life is. When I was four, Barney and his friend Dora, they explained my life. I grew older and I understood life wasn't as nice and caring as I'd expected. There is cruelty, darkness and hardship in every corner of everyone's life. Sins exist everywhere, and the worst part is ... is that I like it. I like it when I see people cower in fear or cry. I get a strange rush and I cannot explain it. I don't act mean or intentionally hurt someone. It's just that when someone's hurt, I enjoy it. I've had my share of sadness but not enough to wish it on others. Nothing drastic has happened to me and I'm not sadistic. It's hard to understand, that's why I want to know what life is. After all, if we don't know what we're doing, how are we doing it?

'Come for dinner,' my mother calls out to me. She works in a huge company somewhere and provides the money. That's all I care about really. I go downstairs to our somewhat decorated living room. The curtains are bright golden, to bring light into the house; the ornaments are from places around the world. They're not my souvenirs, they're my dad's. He's been everywhere. He's even gone to the Amazon River, and to every continent. He's isn't here right now, he's in Peru (third time there). My mom looks sufficiently relieved to see me for some reason. 'Listen, Julie, I'm going to my book club meeting. I'll be back around eleven. I know you'll be sleeping then, so I won't disturb you. Just leave the door unlocked,' she says and then points to the fridge. 'There are some noodles.'

I nod at her and we stare at each other and I silently accept that she would rather spend time with her friends. 'Bye!' I say as she walks on to the pavement. She stumbles a little, her new heels must hurt; how she struggles to fit in with her friends.

Today is Sunday, tomorrow Monday. I groan audibly. I hate Mondays; you just have to make it through the next five days. After that the prize is too light. The weekend isn't some huge revelation about life and every day gets boring. I know everyone else is also bored but I can't live like this. With everything so boring and uninteresting...

I go back to my room without touching the noodles. They must be from Ming-Su and I hate Ming-Su. In my room, I search for my most prized possession – a black permanent marker. It's

42

how I tell myself things. Any word that pops into my head goes on my body. The words are everywhere and written so many times that some are barely visible.

Others cut or scratch themselves because they feel they're not good enough. I write on myself. I am careful to maintain boundaries so the school won't notice. I can only write on my thighs, torso and arms. I cover my arms with long sleeves. But no self-harm. Nothing tragic has happened to me, so how can I say I hate life? I don't hate life; I just don't enjoy it.

I stay up till twelve, online. I don't say anything in the chats, instead, I watch others converse. They notice me and call me out, but I don't say anything. I obviously don't hear the click of the door at eleven. My mom usually comes back the next morning. I've read a lot of books but none so interesting that I stay up all night to discuss it. I seriously want to know the name of this book. I fall asleep at twelve, hoping that this Monday will bring the seeds of change.

My alarm clock rings at exactly seven-thirty. School starts at eight and I always reach at eight-thirty. All my teachers have accepted that I won't be there for the first thirty minutes. They don't say anything, just purse their lips. My first class is art, so I come in even more leisurely than usual. The art teacher does what is expected from him and then packs his bags to leave because the bell has rung. On his way out, I can only hear him mutter, 'Not living up...'

I know what he's talking about. He's talking about my name. You know Shakespeare's most famous character? Yeah, that's my name. With a name like Juliet, everyone expects me to have her gentle nature and then I bring out my reckless crazy. What they don't know is that under that raging storm a calm sea waits ... Juliet! Whose lover, Romeo, died thinking Juliet was dead. Then Juliet woke up to find him dead so she killed herself. Stupidest plot ever! Why would you kill yourself for love? Love is irrational and it destroys life. I mean, some people might be ready to lay down their lives for love. We have a name for those kinds of people – fools.

I meet a friend after the first few classes. We stand near the forgotten lunch hall, away from curious eyes. This lunch hall burnt down a few years ago, but then the school rebuilt it. No one ever uses it, they're afraid of ghosts. See, during the fire, two people died, one of them my friend, but that doesn't give me a reason to mope. Her family is allowed to cry for her but I have to go on.

'Bunsen didn't mind you being late?' asks Marsha, blowing smoke. She holds her cigarette with a huge amount of pride. Marsha is sort of a good girl gone bad. Her dad is this insanely rich billionaire but she never sees him. She smokes as much as she breathes.

'No, he never minds. All of them have gotten used to it,' I say, high-fiving her.

She smirks and then twists her mouth into a heart, trying to make smoke rings. 'There's a new guy,' she says, choking. I don't panic because she always chokes on cigarettes.

'Who is he?' I ask, disinterested.

She smiles and pulls at my brown locks. 'He's got a name that could rival yours,' she says and runs to class.

I don't move. So his name is probably Einstein or Edison. That must be annoying; people will expect him to be smart. I hope he's dumb, then I can laugh as he struggles to cope.

On my way to class I meet Oliver. Oliver is one of my good friends but even he jokes about my name. 'Hey, Juliet! I got news for you,' he says, his eyes shining.

'I know, there's some guy whose name could rival mine,' I say, keeping my voice monotonous.

He nods vigorously. 'He's my cousin, twice removed.' I smile at the thought of another scrawny, geeky and funny copy of Oliver. 'He likes wrestling,' says Oliver, snapping me out of my thoughts. A scrawny and geeky kid who likes … wrestling? 'No, he doesn't look like me,' says Oliver, almost as if he can read my mind.

I flash him a thumbs-up. 'Let's see if this kid is cool enough to hang with us,' I say, trying not to smile.

'He doesn't look like a kid,' mutters Oliver, but he agrees. 'I have free periods afterwards so I'm fine with it.'

I grin guiltily. 'I have a math test next, so skipping is the obvious option.'

Oliver sighs. 'I can teach you the Pythagoras theorem if you want…'

I interrupt him, 'A squared plus B squared equals C squared.'

He gazes at me in wonder and then starts offering profound apologies. I brush them aside and he goes in to ask the new guy.

See, what we do is that we ask newcomers to ditch school and go into the forgotten lunch hall with us. No one has ever

45

said yes. Mostly because they're scared of vengeful ghosts or a teacher catching them. I sit cross-legged by the lunch hall, not even considering the possibility of this new guy coming. And, as I expected, Oliver walks to me alone after a while.

'Did he wet his pants?' I ask, laughing.

Suddenly a tall figure sweeps in front of me and I frown. This could only be the new guy; no one else would come this close to the lunch hall.

'You're Juliet, right?' he asks, eyes mint-green, hair swept to a side. His voice is deep with a curious catch in places.

'And apparently you have a name that could rival mine,' I say staunchly. 'You scared? There might be ghosts?'

He merely shrugs. 'I learned long ago that ghosts live in your mind.'

I stare at him for a second because that actually makes sense. Then I grimace. 'Come in, then.'

He follows Oliver and me as we step into the dark lunch hall. The chairs and tables are all covered with white cloth, like in a ghost-house. But no burning smells, no spirits come out to kill us. Walls striped with yellow flowers, so it's ironic how people are scared of this place. I look up at him to see his expression. It's apathetic, unconcerned and, to sum it up, bored. 'You're bored?' I ask without thinking.

'It's not much, is it? I was hoping for something spookier,' he says, looking around. His face remains impassive and unreadable.

'You know, you're the first person to come in here without crying,' I tell him.

46

He smiles, apologetic. 'I guess I've seen a lot, so this isn't the worst.' I feel uncomfortable at this open invite into his life.

'Uh, guys, I'm here too, you know,' says Oliver nervously.

I ignore him and sit on the floor.

'Afraid of the chairs?' asks the new boy, taking a chair from under the sheets.

I get up, viciously grab a chair and slam myself down on it. Then, to make a point, I say, 'Happy?'

He nods and pats my back. 'Very.'

We sit in silence for a while and my watch reads two-fifteen. School ends at three, so forty-five minutes to go. 'What do you like to do?' I ask him. 'Except wrestling, of course.'

'I hate wrestling,' he says and gets an 'oh' from me.

'So what do you like to do?'

'I like to read, write … and study.'

There goes the Einstein dream. 'Let me rephrase that: what are you good at?'

'I'm not the best judge of what I'm good at.'

'Those are other words for I'm not good at anything,' I say.

'I'm good at studies, sport, art and really everything,' he says, grinning widely. 'What are you good at, Juliet?'

I wince at my name but say, 'Nothing.'

He looks at me weirdly. 'Everyone can do at least one thing. Everyone has a purpose but whether they fulfil it is up to them.'

I sigh. 'Did you make that up?' I ask.

He smiles sheepishly.

'I'm really not good at anything. I cannot draw or write well. I'm tall, so sport should be easy, but is not…' I suddenly trail off. I mentally slap myself. How can I possibly be telling a perfect stranger everything about myself? 'I have to go,' I say and rush out of the lunch hall.

I suddenly gasp – Oliver was my ride home and he's still in there. No, he's coming out now.

Oliver jogs up to me. 'Y-you r-ran out. C-come, I'll give you a ride.'

I smile at him gratefully. I hate how people are nice to me and yet I imagine them trapped in a box, wailing.

Back home, I have the burning desire to write something on myself. I take my marker and write *secrets* over my left arm. Below it I see *away, gone, mourning, death* and so many others. As I lay my head on the pillow, I remember something; no one told me the new boy's name.

I moan through the first three periods, not paying attention. The teachers make the lessons absolutely dull and that complies with the rest of my life. I wait hungrily for break-time so I can ask him his name. Could it really rival mine? Juliet is such a tip-of-the-tongue name and yet no one uses it. Is his name Alva, Archimedes, Artichoke? I don't know! Why why why didn't I ask him his name yesterday?

'Miss Bol?' asks the English teacher. I stand up. He shakes his head. 'I asked you: what is assonance?'

I bite my lip, trying to remember. I know it's a device used in poetry but I don't see its importance. Shouldn't poetry come from the inside and not from rules? 'Assonance is when the pronunciation of vowels in a sentence sounds the same.' I smirk.

'Care to give us an example?'

'The snake's hiss was a near miss, my dear sis,' I say and a few kids laugh.

The teacher's face shrinks but he doesn't say anything. He can't because my example isn't wrong.

When the bell rings, I'm ecstatic. I finally get to conquer the unknown. I whizz out of class but am stopped by Marsha. She's still holding a cigarette and blowing smoke.

'Don't you ever actually go to class?' I ask, waving away the smoke.

'They don't know I even go here,' she says, coughing. 'My dad writes me letters asking about my GPA so I can take over the company, but I don't want to do business, I want to paint.' Marsha might smoke all the time but she can paint. Meanings multiply behind every stroke. If she wasn't already inheriting millions, I'd say she could become a millionaire with her paintbrush.

'Right, have you met the new guy?' I ask her, still waving at the air.

'Yeah, he's pretty cool. He doesn't smoke, so that's bad. You should smoke...' Marsha suddenly gasps for breath before staggering off somewhere. Tarring your lungs can have side-effects.

After twenty minutes, I find the new boy sitting with Oliver on the fence that surrounds the school. Oliver passes him some cheese and he smiles, content.

'You like cheese?' I ask, coming into view.

Oliver looks surprised at seeing me but the new boy doesn't. He says, 'I like cheese.'

'Which cheese do you hate?' I ask.

Oliver gets up. 'Before you guys start doing your creepy thing, I'm going back to class.' I ignore him, knowing how much he doesn't want that. 'Okay, here I go,' he says and walks slowly out.

'Blue cheese,' says the new boy.

I feel compelled to ask, 'Why?'

'Blue cheese should be blue, but it's not. I hate things that say they're something but are not,' he says, face hardening a little.

'So you must hate Iceland and Greenland then?' I say jokingly.

'I do,' he says firmly. 'Aren't you going back to class?' he asks after a while.

'No. Are you?'

'My English teacher's a bore … Juliet, let's go to the woods.'

It's a statement, so I treat it like one. Together we march on to the road. Across the school is an abundance of plants, growing so long they've turned into a forest. We follow the narrow dirt road into the wilderness. We don't say a word until we're safely in the heart of the woods. The trees and shrubs are all close-knit and there is a huge canopy above. Birds and squirrels chirp, while a river gurgles nearby. We lie on the green grass, tall enough to dance in the breeze.

'You know it's against the rules to be here? We could get expelled,' I say, even though I already know what he's going to say. Either *rules are meant to be broken* or *what's life without a little danger?* He chooses the latter and I grin at him.

Then he suddenly asks, 'Do you like your name?'

'No, isn't it obvious?'

'Why?' he asks like he's interested.

Such a clear-cut question, but I can't think of anything to say. People know that I hate my name but nobody ever asked why. 'People expect me to be this unforgettable character from an undying book. Instead they get me, crazy retard Juliet. You know…'

'… I know.' His eyes are soft.

I give a harsh laugh. 'How would you know?'

He looks slyly at me. 'I would know because I have a name that could rival yours.'

'What is it?' I ask, finally ready to know. The moment of anticipation, expectation before he tells me is infinite. It's like when you're on the tip of a roller-coaster or just about to receive your exam paper. I don't know why his name is of such great interest to me. I guess I just want to have an equal; someone who's gone through the same humiliation as me. I know the humiliation is all in my head but, after all, doesn't Satan live inside our minds?

'Tell me,' I say when he doesn't speak.

'You really want to know?' he asks, a cruel air to him.

I nod.

'Fine.' He smiles a bit. 'My name is Romeo and I'm pleased to make your acquaintance, Juliet.'

I stare at him for what feels like an eternity. 'Romeo?' I ask after a few minutes. He doesn't look at me but I can feel his smugness. 'So your parents like Shakespeare too?' I ask.

He half-sits up. 'Liked. My dad used to love Shakespeare. Then he died. My mom isn't ... all there. She tells the future for a living and we get along only with my scholarships.' He scowls. 'She could try but she insists on living with the dead. They're dead, let them stay forgotten.'

I'm not sure but I think there are tiny tears in his eyes. But the tears don't fall. His eyes soon return to their normal state. 'Let's just stay,' he says and holds my hand. It's not a romantic gesture, it's a sign of friendship. I know there's a deeper meaning to his *let's just stay*. However, I don't wish to explore it. I just want to stay lightly, relaxing in this while. Otherwise my mind is a steam engine whose accelerator is always on. So we lie on the bright grass, staring at the canopy overhead. We don't say a word, not wanting to ruin the silence. We just stay.

I don't know how long we lie there but I finally break the silence. It's like drawing a sword into ice. 'We need to go,' I say hurriedly but Romeo doesn't move. I nudge him and he opens his eyes.

'Why ... why can't we just morph into trees? Then we will remain.'

I sigh deeply; he was obviously going to hit me with another question. 'No one is meant to last forever, Romeo. Let's get back to school.'

He grins crookedly and holds his hand out, pointing to his wrist. 'That'll be hard to do – it's six.'

'You might get into trouble. It's just your second day.' I try to sound concerned even though I'm not.

'What about you?'

'They don't care about me. I'm a failure.'

His eyes widen. 'You mean they never scold you?'

'I think they're tired of shouting at me.'

'Lucky!'

'I guess in a way hate is luck. I like luck so I like hate,' I say figuratively.

'You're whimsical,' he compliments me.

I smile at him and we make our way out of the woods. We get on to the narrow road between the woods and our school. We both smell of dirt and we have snail goo squashed on to our skin. Our clothes are torn and I have gashes and cuts all around. Our aroma is of sweat. Yet I've never felt cleaner.

I reach home before Mom is back. She usually returns late, around eight, and it's seven now. I quickly wash my body, except the ink. That permanent marker really is permanent and I like it that way. Just as I sit down to listen to music, I hear the door click. Someone's home.

'Juliet, I got you a treat!' she calls, her voice high and happy. I sigh, realizing she is drunk.

'What is it?' I ask wearily.

'I got you a book!' she says excitedly and comes into view. The smell of alcohol hits me.

'Which one?' I ask her.

'*Romeo and Juliet.*'

I wince at the title. She knows I hate my name, why would she get me a book that will taunt me? 'Thanks, Mom, just lay off the booze next time,' I say.

She giggles and runs off to her room.

I go up to my room and find my marker. *Changing* and *feather* are inscribed on my legs. Just before I fall asleep, I turn on a mix of songs that soothe me. And just before I close my eyes I whisper, 'Thank you.' I don't know whom I say it to but I mean it.

I wake up sick and groggy. School is not a place I want to go to every morning. The teachers have anyway accepted that I won't attend their classes, so what could happen if I miss the classes completely? I could just escape to the great infirmity of the woods. The woods could be my salvation from my lack-of-fun life. I'm having a deep rebellious moment and I don't want school to spoil it. There's a difference between learning in school and actually learning. School judges, decides and forces you to memorize. In really learning, in discovering knowledge, there is complete and utter bliss. I look down at my skin, which literally screams words. I hate having to maintain only a small part where I can write. I want to fill my whole skin with words.

The morning is dark and the sun can barely be seen. Mist hangs in the air and the air is cold. I like the cold. No one asks why I'm wearing a jacket. It also gives me an adrenalin rush that the sun cannot bring. The sun is warm, cheerful and beautiful; everything I'm not. I groan all the way to school, kicking stones out of the way. When I reach the huge steel main gates, I'm greeted by Marsha. The usual cloud of smoke surrounds her and she's still coughing and wheezing. 'You're early,' she says in her raspy voice. 'It's only eight.'

'Your face was something I had to see,' I quip.

She laughs, but not at my joke; she's always like that. She's not a serious person, but she has serious thoughts. I like people who think. 'Do you ever take off that jacket? I swear I've never seen your arms.'

You're lucky then, I feel like saying. 'I like this jacket, it's comfortable.'

'When's your dad coming back?' she asks and I'm surprised to see that she wants to know.

'Maybe next week … I don't know,' I say and look at the cars on the road.

'I like smoke,' she adds randomly when she sees Oliver approaching us. He runs up to us, breathing hard.

'Where's Romeo?' I ask nonchalantly.

Oliver and Marsha both smirk at me knowingly. 'I see you discovered his name,' Marsha says, her lips still carved into a smile.

'He's not coming today,' answers Oliver.

'Why?' I insist, curious. It's been a really long time since I felt curious. When I was eleven, my parents and I would go to the lake near our house. It wasn't a great lake, actually it was polluted and fish died in there. The garbage there, left by humans of course, was endless. However, I liked it. Those days, my dad would never be home and my mom was always busy. So our family picnics at the lake were something to strive for. We would sit together and feed the dying fish. Because we were creating a memory. That's all everyone wants. They want to create memories.

'He said he wants to see some band opening,' Oliver says, not really paying attention.

'Which band?' I persist.

'Some weird band called Rudimental. He says their album release is happening, so he's trying to get tickets.'

'Where is it?'

'I'm not sure but Romeo's leaving at twelve, so he's not coming to school today. Why?' asks Oliver, turning to look at me.

But I'm already making my way to Oliver's house. Rudimental is one of my favourite bands and the thought of going to their album release ... there are infinite possibilities. Oliver lives in a sunny house at the start of Summer Street. However, the damp, misty weather dulls his house's halo. The curtains which are bright red are pulled apart, showing they have nothing to hide. And they don't. Oliver has the most normal life you could live.

'Hello,' I say as someone opens the door. It's Oliver's mom. She's a round lady who loves baking and knitting and her son is the most precious jewel to her. So she obviously doesn't approve of the girl who taught her son things darker than banana cake.

'Juliet, what a ... pleasant surprise,' she says, pursing her lips.

'I'm here to meet...' I don't know whether to say Romeo because it will just sound really weird, '... Oliver's cousin.'

She looks back into her neat living room, where Romeo sits on the couch, headphones on, lost to the world. 'Funny, he didn't mention visitors,' she says, trying to get rid of me.

But I'm not one to be shooed away. 'Really, he told me to come for tickets to a music concert. He's going at … what did he say now, oh yes, twelve, and I'm supposed to accompany him,' I lie perfectly.

She doesn't doubt me for a second, although she obviously wishes she could. 'Romeo, Juliet is here to go with you for those tickets,' she says and strides over to the kitchen, where the smell of baking is evident. Romeo looks stunned to see me but recovers easily.

'I didn't know I was giving you a ticket,' he says and pats the space next to him.

'If you can get one. Do you know how hard it is to go to an album release?' I ask him as I sit down.

'Yeah, but it's Rudimental, no one really listens to them,' he says, slightly amused to see me at his doorstep. I snort at his ignorance and turn away, not bothering to reply.

'So people listen to Justin Bieber?' I ask as a joke.

He takes it seriously. 'Haven't you heard of Beliebers?'

'That's not real music,' I protest.

'To you,' he retorts.

'Whatever. Let's just get tickets to Rudimental,' I say, letting my irritation show.

He notices it because what he says next makes me thump his back, thrilled and suddenly energized. 'I already got tickets,' he says, grinning at my eager face.

I laugh, happy. 'How?'

'Some things are better left unsaid.' At that moment I don't care how he got tickets except that, well, he got tickets to Rudimental! 'Thank you,' I say, truly meaning it.

'Who says I'm taking you?' he asks.

'*Yeah, but it's Rudimental, no one really listens to them.* I quote you word to word. So in conclusion, no one else will go,' I counter.

He smiles. 'Sunday night. I'll pick you up at eight.'

I smile back at him and suddenly there's too much happiness in the room. 'Bye,' I say and leave abruptly. I rush out of his house, unable to process what just happened. I hate what I was and what I'm becoming. I used to be a dark monster whose life was a huge non-event. I'm becoming a person who cares, a person who feels real emotion and behaves normally. And like a child I feel like saying, *I don't want to change.*

I spend the next few hours at a nearby café, simply staring at the horizon. Not thinking, not feeling. Just lying in my skin and staying. Being who I am. The waitresses notice me but they don't say anything. It's not every day you see someone with such a calm expression sitting in a café. They probably think I'm a Buddhist-to-be or a preacher of non-violence. I don't order anything but simply stay. I want to tell someone this: *Right now, I am thankful to be alive.*

I feel back to normal once I am home again, thank god. At night I carve *memory* and *remain* with my most prized possession. My mom obviously doesn't notice, she never does. No one does.

The next few days pass in a blur. I go to school but it's like I'm not really there; instead, I'm floating. I've often felt a sense of weightlessness, but now I feel like I don't exist. Still, I go through what my life is – school. I make it to Saturday without any problem but I don't contact Marsha or Oliver. They're sort of the only friends I have. I had another friend, but she died in the fire, remember? But I'm not allowed to feel sorry for her.

The clock reads seven-thirty and I'm pacing the hallways. Mom is out doing … her book club. I don't know what it is that she does and I don't care. My legs feel like they've walked for ages and, really, it seems like one minute is equivalent to a lifetime. I'm really excited about this concert and there's nothing that can stop me from going. Except an avalanche or a hurricane or if I *die*. Rudimental is my favourite techno band and going to their album release is a dream come true, plus it means that something will have finally *happened* in my life. Something I can have an emotion about, because nothing has really happened to me before. I'm just a weird girl called Juliet with some dark thoughts about life; nothing tragic or extraordinary has ever happened to me. So I don't have an excuse for writing all over myself. But now something's going to happen. I'm going to create a *memory*. The doorbell finally rings at one minute past eight. I shake my head at Romeo's stupidity. He should have known my door is always open, because no one knows when my mom or dad will get home.

'Ready?' he asks.

'Ready,' I confirm. He leads me to his hired car and we relax in the backseat. The drive is fairly normal until I get *the phone call*. It's from an unknown number, so I don't know if I should pick up or not.

'H-hello,' says a watery voice. Mom's? There seems to be a lot of bustle in the background, judging from the noise.

'Hello,' I say back.

'Listen, darling, can you come to Millington Hospital? S-something bad has happened.' She sounds distressed and her voice seems to break like she's trying not to cry. Did something happen to her?

'What's wrong?' I ask.

'It's – it's your dad,' she says sobbing and cuts the phone.

I scowl. It's just like her to not tell me anything. Dad? Dad isn't even here unless … I entertain the worst possible theories of what happened to him. I gulp loudly and Romeo notices.

'Something wrong?'

'M-my dad's in the hospital,' I say, trying to keep my voice even. It works because I know exactly how to keep my emotions inside me.

'Do you want me to take you there?'

'Yes. You could leave after dropping me. Just give my ticket to some homeless guy…' My voice trails off. I so badly wanted to go to this event, I was going to create a memory.

'Sure,' he says and doesn't argue. I was expecting him to.

We reach the hospital in an hour, assuming that it was an hour. It could have been more, I don't know. I rush through the wards, not knowing if Romeo has left or whether I should check the reception. There are no tears in my eyes and I fight to keep steady. Luckily, I run into my mother carrying some water. She's with nurses and a doctor. Her hair is pulled up into a ponytail and her eyes are red.

'What happened, Mom?' I ask, approaching her.

The doctor exchanges glances with a nurse. Mom sobs, unable to speak, and motions to a nurse.

The nurse's voice is firm yet gentle, kind but not nurturing. 'Your father was in an accident.'

'Is he okay?' I ask, not letting my face leak anything.

She exchanges glances with the doctor again. 'No, he, uh, he *died.'*

My mother sobs even louder now and people give me sympathetic nods. Romeo is nowhere to be seen. The doctor and the nurses wait to see my reaction. I don't say or do anything. I can't let them know I'm hurt, I can't let them know I'm weak. I don't know what to do or where to go. My pillar, the man who goes everywhere, is dead? He cannot be dead; nothing like this has ever happened before. Sure, my grandparents died, but that was different: I wished for their death. I was a small girl then and it seemed like they hated me, so I wished for their death. It happened a few days later and I had a guilty conscience for a while. I recovered because I knew it wasn't my right to be upset.

I run out of the hospital in a mad dash because I can't stay there. My mom yells my name but even she's in a lot of grief. I run down the street, not knowing where I'm going. I try to hail a taxi, but no car stops. I see an underground tunnel and then it disappears. A camel walks by and asks if I want a ride ... Now I'm hallucinating. The shock is getting to me and the busyness of the street doesn't help. I feel dizzy and I need ... I need ... Suddenly a black car whizzes by and it seems familiar because it is. It's Romeo's car.

He gets out and quickly grabs me before I faint. I don't register much except blurs. No, I'm letting feelings get to me. I have to be stronger. I force my mind to concentrate, to stay in one place and understand what's going on. I make sure I'm not crying or yelling and I tune into what Romeo's saying. He just says Shivered Hill and gets a grunt in return. Shivered Hill? But that's the forest near my school ... We drive on in silence and I don't move a muscle. That includes the muscles near my eyes, so no tears are formed. He grabs me again, but it's gentle and a low thank-you is muttered. We get out of the car and I can make out only the dark silhouette of the evergreen forest. Romeo leads me up a familiar trail and then we stop. He lays me down on the familiar bright grass and I stare up at a familiar canopy.

'You're here,' he says and it's all I need to know.

That I'm here.

I SIT AS INNOCENCE

I sit as flesh, alive and solid. I sit as skin, draped over my body. I sit as lips, mouth, hands, legs; pale, only sitting, unmoving, unwanting.

The room is empty and its windows are boarded; I am sealed from the outside and nobody is anywhere to be seen. I can see a body, mine alone, everyone else is gone. I do not care, I like it so, all me, all me, always alone.

A shallow pond in the wild, light laughter, the smile of a child, an enriched lake of time's young years – the memories I hold dear.

A lover's quarrel this place has known; fights, make-ups and changes of tone.

It's been my first, my last, in my homeless nights when I roamed the country, fuelled by might.

But now this body's old and weary, it can't walk, let alone hold steady, so this place so close to my heart will be the end of my start.

Let's play a game you can never win, I'll be the master and you my sin. In an enigmatic play of shadows, where fantasies lie behind every page. But, of course, there will be danger — your body will shriek, your hands will bleed, your eyes will drip, my venom alight, your heart will fail, exhausted. Your soul will scream and, with your last breath shallow and mournful, I will warn you that death never came with a warning. And then, my dear, you will die.

Roses are red and pretty, with drooping, lilting bows the colour of spilt blood, I do adore them so. Prickly thorns and murderous rage stored inside my pretty rose. A single touch and all fall prey and their ichor is spilt below, oceans of coward red. Never mind, my blood has been spilt before.

Fathomable. The first thought in my mind when I saw you. Your eyes did not hold the rage of the wind and your body did not draw my soul forth. You did not remind me of sugary evenings and chocolate stares. You did not make me feel powerless and powerful all at once. You did not make me feel every happy memory I'd ever had. You did not ever make me feel even content. But you made me feel. And that is why I love you. Not because you showed me sights I'd never seen before but because you taught me how to love them. And I forgave you when you loved me.

From where do you hail, girl with the guarded mouth? What secrets do you hold that I, even in my old age, cannot? I see desperation bleed out of your veins and loss drip down your eyes. A heartless love had captured you and now you're empty enough to turn to my lies.

Your hands are purple and blue but those thoughts must be fading now. Come, girl, come closer, feel my decaying breath. Watch me heave through my immortal days, as I take all those who are done. Girl, let down your crystal armour and let me take you to the depths from where I hail.

Have you ever had a dream, a simple wish among the stars, a wild jump into the unknown, the need to go away far? Have you ever had a dream that made you stop and think of leaving this life which held you close, and starting anew? Have you ever had a dream, which seemed so reckless at first, but then that dream grew and grew until it consumed you?

The thorn-mingled bark of green which stands unyielding, a warrior to touch. Amidst a secret garden, a garden of evil, lying near a stone river. The crunch of fallen leaves like the shredding of paper, two feet in worn black soles, arms sudden and kneading my forehead, slow breaths warning.

A garden of evil, the warm mellow light now bitter and blinding, fingers pressed down on my neck, teasing, pinching, contracting, collapsing. A last glance at innocence, the loveliness of carving letters on wood: it takes two feet to lose my purity.

My heart lies nestled in the coils of the branches in the woods we lost, it caresses the rough bark, it trusts the trunk to protect it, to keep it hidden from harm. My arms are buried in the fallen leaves snipped at odd places, spreading through the veins, forming a web of cotton string, stretching out through the midrib, reaching the apex. My body lies on the ground, uncontained and scattering through sand the colour of broken tiles, the cracks in the course floor my own curves, creating a coliseum of crevices from which I spring.

The sky is too large. The air guzzles and bubbles before rising up, swirling and gushing into the large blue, withering and dithering before the attack, my body the bridge through which the air reaches the sky.

I am the messenger, I am the taker of talk, the carrier of creation, the giver of glory. I am the angel of grief, I see the pain and I swallow it, so it cannot blunder and blast and bellow at the one deserving of it. I am the angel of grief, I am the keeper of the faith, the one who blinds them so they can love, the only one who can see. I am the saviour who grieves for those I save.

What's in the water?

He sits on my knee like a child, bobbing up and down, content in the water as I push him into it, his hands the paddles and his mind the tide beckoning him along. What's in the water, he says again, but now he is a man, and the water has started its retreat from him, he is losing his vitality, the water is losing its moisture.

What's in the water, the old man asks me, as if I might know more than him, for I have touched it, I have left it; and he thinks he is special when he says, Why was I taken from the water?

I know I knew the answer, but I know I have forgotten. The sea was open but so was the bottom.

At night, everything is in darkness. Black, infinite and dead, but I have to confess, I've never been better in my head.

The dark fuels my happiness. It's a scam, a façade. I get tricked; I think I've escaped the mess, the mess that I've made.

Everyone's curtains are drawn, no one looks outside…

But it's all a con. For in the dark everyone confides. The night stays awake with us. In turn, the night is the one we trust.

I'm standing on this slow-moving ship, watching the lights across the Parisian harbour – mothers coming into bedrooms, fathers whispering on the other side of the doors. Through the windows I can see each family traipsing around, garrulous and excited. I have to remember, though, that I will always be on the outside, looking in.

The wind comes in from the east as I struggle to tame the beast that is constantly raging and roaring, bellowing and moaning; it won't stop clawing and biting. Yet, of it there's never been a sighting. For it is what is killing me, it is that which can see everything I am. My name, my life and all my plans. Can't you see? What is killing me is me.

MEETING THE ANOMALIES

MEETING THE ANOMALIES

It had seemed perfect. We'd recently moved to a new apartment on the outskirts of the city. My parents' workplaces were close by, so the move made their lives a little easier. Our little apartment was quite sweet; lovely white furniture that looked like it came from a magazine. The walls were cherry pink and the cupboards absolutely white. The apartment building was well maintained and whitewashed every twelve months. The apartment complex's name was Whispering Winds and after a night, we found out why. The trees would make a lovely *pssst* sound when the wind blew through them. Our neighbours were kind, friendly and well mannered. 'This is the place we've been looking for,' my mum had said to my dad and he'd smiled.

Then we met them. They were three ladies, very, very different from the kind of people we'd met until then. Our other neighbours had gentle, caring voices with satisfactory appearances.

These three ladies all looked the same. They had the same big nose with a huge grey wart on it. When they stood in the sun, their faces had a green tinge. Everyone at Whispering Winds called them the 'anomalies'.

One fine morning, after I'd had my breakfast and said goodbye to my parents, the doorbell rang. I ran to the door, looked through the eyehole and gasped. The three ladies were there! Not wanting to be rude, I opened the door and uttered a nervous, 'Good morning.'

One of the ladies smiled, showing her yellow teeth, and said, 'Good morning, Ali. We've come to welcome you to this place.'

I nodded, my mind reeling. I'd never met them before and yet they knew my name. Before I could respond, the same lady began to talk again. 'I'm being terribly rude by not introducing myself. My name is Heath, and these two are Feather and Light.'

I nodded again; this trio looked exactly the same, so how was I to tell them apart?

'Ali, I'm being terribly rude but do you by any chance have tea?' asked Feather or Light.

'I have some in a pot, I'll bring it for you,' I mumbled, barely audible.

I quickly fetched the tea, for the sooner they drank, the sooner they'd leave. I carefully poured it into four cups and the three ladies picked up their drinks. Before any of us could drink, one of the ladies brought out a white packet which had no label on it.

'Ali, drink your tea with some of this, it's magical,' she commanded sweetly.

I knew better than to accept eatables from strangers but when she put it in all of our cups, I decided to try it. The powder was dark green and when I drank it, it tasted like ambrosia, the drink of the gods.

'Now you're one of us,' cackled one of the ladies and quick as lightning, they were gone.

I let out a sigh I didn't know I was holding in. The meeting had gone quite well, I had nothing to worry about. I locked the door and then went to comb my hair.

There was a surprise awaiting me in the mirror. A huge grey wart was growing on my enlarging green nose!

WHEN CARL'S CAFÉ CLOSED ITS DOOR ON ME

My mother had us banned from my favourite coffee shop when I was ten years old. Carl's Café stood atop the filthy grime-covered road on which I often spied cockroaches that everyone in town pretended not to see, because if the best café of our town was infested, the small number of tourists we got each year would vanish.

We usually lost all our business to Ellway, a town marginally bigger than us, a few miles closer to the sea. In most ways, Ellway was no different from our town – it had the same kind of beach bums and meth heads populating it, about the same number of small diners and cafés, a handful of branded storefronts. As for us, we had a GAP the entire town was proud of. And a hotel, which I had never set foot in, but in front of which my mother and I often stood, in the suffocating sun, ice cream dripping down my chin as we watched the large wooden gates sheltered by palm trees open and close, letting out the largest cars our town had ever witnessed. My mother would wallow in the breeze, purse her lips and smile every so often with hope in her eyes and she'd look down at me with her expression glazed, and I knew she was talking but not really to me when she'd say, 'We have everything!' and laugh joyfully, her voice a gentle murmur resembling the chime of the ringing of fake gold bells in Catalina's fashion store. She'd say it so loud sometimes, that the bush from behind which we watched the hotel would attract a sudden look of suspicion from the security guard on duty.

Everything changed when Ellway was chosen as the next big beach destination and a Four Seasons opened there. Instantly, even the few road-tripping families we'd originally grown accustomed to we lost to Ellway and my mother cried, because if our town didn't have any money, she didn't have any money, and she needed money for the grandeur she loved and cherished and so often tried to recreate in the confinement of our dull lives.

The hotel in our town shut down because nobody had any use for it any more, and my mother cried for that too. She spoke of how that hotel was the crux of my childhood, the cherry on top of my everyday life, and I didn't have the heart to mention that we'd never even been inside. It wouldn't have mattered anyway; my mother never heard anything she didn't want to hear.

And then everything got worse. My father, my mother and I lived in a small quarantined neighbourhood, and our house had two rooms and a kitchen. It was covered in pesky houseflies, but my mother persevered and promised that one day we'd move into a real house and be real people. She worked double shifts at the diner next to our house, and charmed anyone who tipped her regularly, because my mother could be quite charismatic; it was the lilt in her voice anytime she spoke, it sounded like she had something worth saying, like you were worth saying something to. She made it sound like she didn't belong in our town, as if she was something more, and she made it sound like you were too. Everyone wanted to sit in her section of the diner, just to hear her speak.

My father never worked – he spent all his time outside our house, and it would be days, weeks and sometimes even months before we even had dinner together. He didn't know my favourite colour and I never bothered to tell him. I didn't know where he went all day or what he was doing, but I knew my mother knew because sometimes she'd call him and scream into the phone and I would hear laughter on the other end – in not only a male voice, but a female one as well. And then a week after the closing of the hotel, my father took his packed bags, gave my mother one last kiss, nodded to me and walked out with a woman who lived in the building opposite ours. (Sometimes I'd see her at eleven in the night, sitting on the sidewalk with her only pair of wobbly high-heeled boots to her side, smoking.) Later, my mother grudgingly told me that they'd gone to Ellway to start a new life.

I wanted to ask why, why did Daddy leave us, but I knew if I asked my mother, her face would crack and she'd cry for hours, so I didn't say anything and my mother didn't say anything, and the next day she went to work, and she smiled and laughed and chattered with the crowd, but nobody noticed that her eyes were lifeless and her laugh too high-pitched to be genuine. Everything seemed exactly the same as it had always been, except it wasn't.

Three days after my father left, my mother was told to take a paid holiday due to the rough patch she was going through. She'd smiled and looked at me and said, as if sensibly, 'It's not really going to be any different,' and I'd smiled back because she was right. I'd rarely see my father before he'd left, and I was never going to see him again. That woman could have him (maybe he'd buy her a new pair of heeled boots which didn't wobble as much) as long as I had my mother.

My mother told me she'd take me out for a treat and we'd go to a big fancy restaurant and order an entrée, a main, a side dish, a dessert, and we'd tip the waiters and wear our best dresses and act like celebrities. Of course, I knew that meant she'd wear her new lipstick and we'd go to any coffee shop nearby and order an extra cupcake.

My mother didn't know that though. She really believed her own lies, and when we walked out of our shoebox of a house towards my favourite coffee shop, I was ecstatic as was the nature of a ten-year-old girl allured by food, and I didn't pay attention to how my mother's eyes glazed over as we settled down in the familiar embrace of the chairs of Carl's Café, and how a desperate, vicious grin appeared on her cracking face. Her fingers sparked as she leafed through the menu, and when I finally ordered a large steak and ice cream (my mother refused to order; another thin-lipped smile, the condescending 'no, thank you' that put people off), she hissed at me, and I finally saw the rising fire in her eyes.

I remembered listening to my parents arguing once, my father's bellowing, raging voice, my mother's tear-filled words of martyrdom. My father was angry because some of the townies had heard my mother say that this town was a 'waste of space in the middle of nowhere producing idiots who only know how to make bigger idiots,' and my mother had defended herself by saying that she was destined for more, that fate would lead her to a life of luxury one day, and my father had sighed and stopped screaming and said, 'Don't you get it? You might not think so, but you're part of this town, you're one of the idiots.'

And the fire would rise in my mother's eyes any time she wanted to prove him wrong. She was obviously bitter about this issue because my father (the heavy-boned no-brainer) had made it out of here, and she, the elegant one of the two, with her fancy accent and great expectations, was still stuck.

The first question out of my mother's mouth was not the one I was expecting. It was only a build-up; I could tell from the nervous frenzy in her voice as she spoke that she was leading up to something. 'Who do you think is prettier, *she* or me?' My mother sat up straight.

The real answer was *she*, for *she* was younger and her hair was blacker and her nails were longer and her face was always painted. But that wasn't completely true, because even though my mother's face had creases and she always looked tired and weary, there was a certain class and grace my mother possessed that *she* would never be able to replicate. My mother always seemed magical, something more.

'You, obviously.'

'Would you do anything for me, anything for your mother? It would be fun, great fun!' My mother's face shone, and the fire started to grow larger and larger.

I swallowed, waited.

'Do you want to do something unscrupulous, something, oh, something simply and utterly debauched?'

I began to eat my steak faster. I wanted to finish it in time.

'Come away then, come away, come, follow me.' There wasn't time to finish the meat because my mother had already pulled me out of Carl's Café and into her world.

We stood in the bushes till closing time when the last waitress locked up and left. Bugs sat in my hair and mosquitoes reddened my calves, and I was sure we had been standing in trash. It was eleven, and there was no one in sight and the streetlights hung miserably in the sudden cold, harsh wind. They flickered on and off and my mother once again pulled me out and in front of the glass doors of Carl's Café.

The fire in my mother's eyes was at the fiercest it had ever been. She also looked the happiest she'd been in a long time. I could see large grey stones at her feet and instantly I knew what she wanted to do. I also knew that there was no point in even trying to stop her. There, on the eve of our banishment from my favourite coffee shop, my mother delivered her soliloquy in pitches of glee and wonder. Her teeth chattered as she spoke in the cold, but the fire in her mind warmed her thoughts. 'We're going to get out if it's the last thing we do. I'll give you a nice life, I promise, one day we'll be real people, in a large mansion with stone-clad walls and a big pool. You like water, don't you?

84

Never mind, I'll hire you ten swimming instructors; oh, and I'll take you to the centre of my glitz and my glamour, and now this is how we get there. We get out of this town, we make sure they throw us out, I'll get us thrown out, my girl, I'll force us to leave. Just you wait and watch what your mother is made of.'

Then she picked up the gathered stones and flung them at the glass walls, which stood almost ironically in front of us. The glass shattered, and I had a few measly throws too, but it was my mother who threw rock after rock, tears streaming down her face, tears of happiness, tears of joy, and I knew she was once again seeing that which wasn't there. The clanging of the glass, the smashing of its shards on the ground, wasn't as voluminous as I'd expected the downfall to be; it was a distant murmur, a background to the rage inside my mother, the rage of unfulfilled dreams. My mother appropriated the glass walls with the power of the fear that she was destined for nothing, she blazed her desperate pleas for greatness, she heaved of tiring failure and disappointment, and I stood, a silent observer but a follower in the night.

There were no alarms that went off (we weren't as fancy as that), but after a hazy ten minutes, Carl appeared screaming, and my mother fainted, and I watched and fainted too.

When we were revived, it was morning. My mother looked as contained and sophisticated as she always did, so much so that I could hardly believe anything had even happened the night before. I'd thought, in the illusion of the darkness of the night, that we'd completely trashed Carl's Café, and that it had disintegrated completely, but later, I learnt that we'd barely broken a part of the glass. Still, even though Carl wasn't taking us to the police, we had been caught doing something we weren't supposed to, something so barbarous that my mother had laughed when Carl had confronted her.

He was furious and told her that she'd made a terrible mistake and that the town would turn its back on her, and that the only refuge she'd find would be outside the town's limits, and he told her that he wanted her to leave and never come near his café again.

Looking back, if we hadn't been caught the day my mother decided to rebel, I would probably be a waitress working at the same café I'd once set out to destroy. And for the sake of complete honesty, I'm glad we got caught, because my mother was right; having the town hate us and turn us out was the best thing to ever happen to us because it forced us to leave. It forced us to start over, it forced us to try for the greatness my mother only ever dreamt about.

Looking back, I am glad I was only ten years old when my mother had us banned from my favourite coffee shop, because I was still young, and my mother made sure I didn't grow up a dead end.

THE WALKERS

They walked on eggshells that cracked like skulls under their mangled, half-bitten feet. They had been walking for days: she had not stopped and neither had he. They walked next to each other, not touching, wavering, never feeling the other's skin, never daring to reach for what the other could bring.

She looked straight ahead: at the dirt-speckled trunk of wood where beetles sat like sugar grains on a countertop, and then at him when he watched the sky translate into a mellow brown, yellow ochre forming after the sun dipped so low he almost touched it.

They walked like soldiers, carrying each other's sorrow to battle, tasting the silence between them and rolling it around on their tongues, each one afraid of speaking, afraid that a single word could remind the other that it was time he returned to the woman back home who was bloated with a belly and unsteady on her knees.

She should have walked faster, there were monsters chasing them, but it was him that she wanted to walk with. He could have fallen behind, he could have gone home, but it was her he wanted to walk with.

As they walked farther through the war, and farther away from home, she smelt of smoke and dust, and when he tried to touch her she turned to ash and slipped between his fingers and fell away from him.

He was a man back home. *I am a boy*, he begged, and asked for the land's forgiveness when she carved their names into a tree she was sure would be burnt.

And she is only a girl, youth rose out of her veins and into his and he forgot about the swollen woman waiting for him at home, and he touched her neck, her lips, her arms; he bathed in the softness he was fighting this war for.

The woman back home waited.

The girl next to him exhaled.

The girl and the boy walked on.

IMPERIUM

Large, overbearing grey clouds drape the evening sky, hiding any ray of light that tries to penetrate them. They choke the wind and suffocate any corporeal form that dares to move too close. They hang heavy, their ends not resembling innocent tufts of a child's cotton candy but instead heaving with a macabre viscosity.

My childhood home, once the site of laughter and naive giggles of honesty, now turned into a locus of desolation and utter silence. The silence is unappealing to this street but nevertheless, it pierces the air and holds on to the atmosphere with unseen severed claws of great strength. The silence is invisible, unheard but irrevocably present. As fresh as a blade of grass and as sharp as a newly bought knife, it plunges into the neighbourhood, dancing and calling to the dark clouds above.

There is a smell. A smell of sour grapes and discarded orange peels, stinking of promises that were never kept, of kisses without warmth, or of simply love – the easiest emotion – which proved futile in the end. There are sounds now too, sounds that had gone unnoticed earlier for they were too soft, too quiet to be heard above the silence. The wave of nostalgia that overtook my thoughts is one I put to rest to better hear the foreshadowing. I concentrate on the sounds; what are they, how did they have enough power to break the silence? It is the sound of a drum roll and the volume grows louder and louder, nearer and nearer until it clutches my body, my spirit and contains me within itself.

I am dazed, to say the least, but the sounds soon envelop me in themselves and I understand they are here to warn me. A burst of colours suddenly illuminate the melancholy sky. Different shades range through the air and highlight objects with no will of their own. I do not know the names of these hues – they are far too incandescent to identify. However, I do know that in their entirety, they are of one form and one form only. They are the form of mania.

I fall; fear breaks the silence entirely and the desperation of the quiet is gone. It is replaced by the insanity of the colours, wild and ready to explore their newly found freedom. I am rolling down the street, gravel suffocates my breath and I know I have to fight these sudden foreign colours, but the colours pull at me, prod at my soul and tease my memories with a resolution I know is not their own. They are fuelled by something more powerful.

I shiver in quiet realization even though the colours hold me prisoner in their midst. I ache for the return of the quiet, of the rigidity of the silence. I fall once more, and I know I will continue falling for they control me, they fill in me wishes of Imperium; they tease me with the scent of sour grapes and discarded orange peels. I am lost in the colours once more, and there I will stay until the silence breaks through again.

When I try to tell someone what happened to me on New Year's Eve in my uncle's house, they are bewildered that I am even telling them in the first place. *Me?* they say and laughter flutters out of their mouths and they try to tell me to calm down as they titter away about how they never knew we were so close. *Listen to me*, I say, but then they turn sullen, they glide away, they don't want to hear me, they don't want to know any more.

I think I choose the wrong people to talk to. But to me there is no one else left except second cousins and long-lost friends; no one else wants to listen to what I have to say.

The way I see it, every conversation with somebody is like a business transaction; no one listens unless they get something in return. Even my mother, who tucks me into bed every night and says *I'll love you no matter what*, doesn't want to listen to me. She is considering her options, weighing the costs and benefits in her mind. On the one hand, her son is a celebrity, making millions each year, he will mention her in his next *Vogue* article, she will be remembered as the mother of the greatest artist of our times. On the other, her daughter has pretty much always been miserable, surly, difficult to entertain. *It is just a tiff*, she said to me when I told her what my brother did, *siblings fight*. She seemed so jovial when she said it, sitting on the counter, perched like a canary, pursed lips, low voice. It seemed almost a crime not to believe her.

Stop being so dramatic, she'd said, *they're just pictures and you look lovely.*

When I tried to call my brother after the pictures went viral on the internet, I assumed he would apologize. Instead, he said, *You wanted to be a model and now you are one.*

When, I asked him, and I knew I was about to cry as my voice sounded heavier and huskier than I wanted, *when in my life had I ever said that?*

I remember a day, he said and cut the call.

Those pictures of me remind me of blood. Thick, lascivious, deep red blood. I was sleeping. We were in my uncle's house and I was tired, I had been writing the entire day and wanted to rest. I clambered into one of the spare rooms and went to sleep. There, I assume, my brother entered and took the pictures.

My mother first yelped when she saw the pictures. Arms and legs indistinguishable, drapes the colour of swollen purple grapes; skin, flesh, lips. I lay there exposed, I looked like art.

My mother was ready to beat my brother, she even sat staring at the pictures until she saw the reviews.

Never have we seen such raw magnetic beauty. It's like the body is telling a story a book never could.

I don't remember my sister in the same way everyone else remembers her. I remember her as pinches on the sides of my thighs at the dinner table, sour breaths in the morning when she would crawl into my bed and whisper to me, her words falling on my face with the gentleness of a spider weaving its first web.

The way that I think everyone remembers my younger sister is by her deformity, but even calling it that is an exaggeration. She was born with a small ball made of skin stuck to her ring finger. It was hardly noticeable; it blended in with the calloused finger behind, but nevertheless she was labelled before she could even speak. My parents tried to remove that small ball of dead skin because they couldn't bear to think that she could possibly be bogged down by something so lifeless, that their second child, their last hope before Dad's vasectomy, could be born with a defect.

I can still see her at age four, her smooth brown hair in two ruffled pigtails, wearing a bright yellow shirt my mother dressed her in and crying because the other kids at school told her she was a freak. My mother stands there, like some sort of hopeless apparition fidgeting with those fingers, and finally kisses that small ugly ball of skin before retreating to my father and talking about meeting a doc the next day for surgery.

But that stubborn ball of skin grew back and sat perched on her ring finger, watching us with a sort of vicious pride. *You can't do it*, it said, *you can't change her.*

My mother took the ball of skin on my sister's ring finger as a sort of personal attack. Your daughter will never marry, it told her. Your daughter's finger will never allow a ring, never allow a man.

In spite of all this, my sister was loved. No one pitied her, the ball of skin did not garner that; everyone liked her. It was impossible not to, especially when you met her for the first time. Clear face, thick eyebrows, eyes wide and crescent-shaped. It was like seeing a wayward child composed of an adult's jaws and cheekbones.

When I think of her though, I cannot see her in the way everyone else does. Eyes twinkling with smooth soft smiles as if she is hoarding a joke you just told.

When my parents speak fondly of her, and they say things like *she had such a sweet face* or *her hair was so beautiful*, I feel a sort of vehemence rise within me that wants to scream *but her eyes were so far apart* or *her eyebrows were so thick* or *once I saw her slap a five-year-old*.

But I cannot; see, it would be a form of sacrilege before her funeral.

ROMEO AND JULIET – II

When I was a little girl, Dad and I used to pore over maps and globes. He'd point out all the places he'd been to and I'd point out all the places I wanted to go to. Then we'd bring out all the souvenirs he'd got me from all the places he'd gone to. It was a sort of tradition and a given that he'd bring me something from all the places he'd visit. It didn't matter what it was, as long as it came from that particular place. He's never forgotten till date and it's one of the only things we do as a family. I'd never given it much thought in the hospital but now it's easier to think. It's quieter. He'd gone to Peru, so maybe he got me something else from there; he'd already gotten me a comb and toothbrush. The calm of being in the forest is suddenly broken when I realize I want to see what he got me.

'The suitcase!' I yell, gasping for breath as Romeo makes sure to hold on to me, keeping me from running.

He pulls me back and gently forces me to sit down, asks, 'What suitcase?'

The sound of his voice has a soothing effect. 'The souvenir,' I say and start thrashing about again. I bite him, punch him and kick him but he doesn't let go. 'I need to get to my father's suitcase!' I say forcefully. Then I stop struggling. 'My dead father's suitcase.' I lie back on the ground and rest but without tears.

When I wake up, a little bit of morning sun is creeping in through the gaps in the canopy. I hear light snoring to my right and see the familiar black curls that had held me all night. 'Wake up!' I say, giggling. I don't know why I feel so happy but I just do. What had happened last night? Romeo shiftily gets up and grimaces when he sees a smile on my face. 'Ro-me-o, ha, that sounds like row me home,' I say cheerfully. He looks surprised by my laughter and then says something that lowers my spirit.

'You know your dad's dead, right?' Then I feel the uncontrollable pain I felt last night and lie back down. My eyes, however, shed nothing.

'I know, but everyone dies.'

He narrows his eyes at me. 'Did you like your father?'

'Yeah.'

'And this is your reaction? Hysterics through the night, a fake happy and then normality? And yet no tears?'

I shrug and suddenly feel angry. Who's he to comment on my way of dealing with woe? 'So if I'm happy it's wrong, but I'm supposed to be sad and cry? Well, get this, *Romeo*, I'm not the same as others. I don't cry or feel sorry for myself, simply because I don't deserve to. My dad dying won't make me cry. I'm strong.'

He glances at me harshly but his voice is not harsh. 'Crying doesn't make you weak, it just means you've been strong too long.'

I sigh in exasperation. 'You don't get it, Romeo, I haven't had anything to be sad about so far. Sure, in my family we virtually ignore one another, my friend died in a fire, some other bad stuff happened and I'm a mean, horrible person but...' I grit my teeth, 'I don't deserve to be sad for things I have control over.'

'You're too strong. Let down your walls, Juliet, let them down and then you'll be fine. Don't close up. It's your life, live it.'

I decide to change the topic. 'Can we go get his suitcase?' I ask. I don't let even an ounce of emotion show through my voice or facial features.

'Why?'

I explain the father-daughter tradition to Romeo and he smiles at the obligatory parts. 'Let's go get your dad's suitcase,' he says and I flash him a quiet thank-you.

It could have been a perfect day after Dad died, except we can't get a cab so we have to walk. Sometimes run.

'Are you participating in the singing competition?' Romeo asks as we jog down the road together. The sun isn't shining to its usual extent; its yellowness reminds me of piss. A few morning joggers wave to us as we pass by. 'I can't sing,' I snort. And it's true. I tried once in the shower and I sounded like a dying whale who'd just seen a turtle it could've eaten if it weren't dying.

'Everyone can sing,' Romeo insists. 'Let me hear you.'

I laugh. 'Believe me, you don't want to,' I say and he lets the matter rest. It's unbelievable that I'm having a normal conversation the morning after my dad died. Pain throbs hard at the back of my head but I grin and bear it. Just like I've always done. This reminds me of a scene from the movie *Madagascar*, 'Just smile and wave, smile and wave.' After a few more kilometres of huffing and puffing, I give up trying to run. There's also a stitch in my side and I stop, heaving for breath. Romeo obviously hasn't broken a sweat yet. He looks more energized than ever.

'You do know that we've only done like three kilometres. That is about twenty-five minutes and you're tired. You've got to improve your stamina.' He grins.

'Don't judge me,' I say, still panting.

'You need to go running more often. How about every morning we go for a short run?'

'Every morning?'

'It'll be fun; besides, you need it. Not that you're fat but you're just really tired.'

I glare at him. 'Fine.'

He gives a low whoop and passers-by stop to give him reproachful looks. I shove him, and before you know it, we're having a playful tussle on the side of the street.

My dad just died and I'm laughing; is that even morally right? After a long jog, three stops included, we finally arrive at Millington Hospital. There's a huge ruckus going on in front of the hospital and my mother is right in the middle of it.

'Mom!' I yell and the crowd surrounding her parts.

Everyone is scowling at me and someone says, 'How could you abandon your mother in her time of need?'

Romeo follows me and doesn't pay any attention to anyone either. 'Hello, ma'am, my name is Romeo, and I have kept your daughter free from harm,' he says, introducing himself.

My mother immediately begins screaming and chiding him. 'You vile creature, you kidnapped my daughter! And you have the nerve to call yourself Romeo! I should have you arrested.' She puts her arm around me in a protective gesture.

I break away from her grip. 'He didn't kidnap me. I willingly went with him because he's my friend. Also, I had to get away ... and his name *is* Romeo. I know the chances of the two of us meeting are little ... but get over it.'

She looks shocked at what I just said. The crowd around us exchange glances. One even whispers that it's a classic love story. 'Fine, but *Romeo*, I don't want you near my daughter ever again,' my mother finally says, using his name as a weapon against him.

'But Mom...' I protest.

'But nothing,' she cuts me short. 'He didn't inform us where you were, so he could be liable as a kidnapper.'

'So sue me,' Romeo deadpans. I know he's joking but my mom obviously assumes the worst.

'I will,' she says and drags me back home.

Once we're home and no one is staring at a girl covered in dirt and a woman who seems to have spent her whole life crying, we sit down. Then the shouting begins. Me against my beloved mother. She obviously can't stop crying and tears roll down her face. I remain expressionless but my voice holds a determined fury.

'Juliet Bol, I have never seen such inexplicable behaviour from you.'

'But I haven't done anything!'

'You ran away from me right after your father's death! You did this the last time too, at your friend's funeral. The one who died in the fire. You need to stop running and realize you can't always run ... Bad things have happened to me but I got through them. You know why? Because I stayed with my family. I surround myself with positive influences; not dark, brooding people like your Romeo.'

'He helps me more than you ever could.' The words leave my mouth before I can stop them. The worst part is that it's true. 'He understands me in a way you never can. I'd rather talk to him about Dad than you. You, you're so ... I can't love you. I'm sorry, I know you love me but I just can't return the love. It's not something I want – you deserve a better daughter. One who really wants to go on those shopping trips. I'm not who you want me to be.'

Then I do something I never thought I'd do. I remove my clothes and let her see all the marks I've made on myself. Her face contorts and yet more tears fall, but when she speaks, she becomes the most furious I've ever seen her. Maybe because I just told her that I hated her and that I wished we weren't in the same family.

'Juliet, if you ever speak to that boy or even go anywhere near him again, I swear to god I will disown you and let you die on the streets. And remember, Juliet, this is the day you have officially lost your mother. And the last thing I will ever say to you as your mother is: wash your dirty body and clean those filthy arms and rid them of the evil you have written on them.'

'That's all I wish for,' I say and run to my room and lock the door. I'm in a sort of frenzy, so I grab the marker from its place and begin to write. *Filth*, *abandon*, *disposed* and *ignored* are all on my skin. I bang my head against the wall. When did my life start dying? I think for a while before I answer my own question: since the day I was born. I've had bad luck and death in me since I was born, so I'm a danger to everyone. What is life? I wonder and lie on my bed, waiting for the tears that refuse to come.

My mother isn't there in the morning. I make myself a quick sandwich and rush to school. No one would expect to see me there, not just two days after my dad's death. But I have to see Romeo. When I see him, I drag him in the direction of the woods. He doesn't object; not that it matters. Oliver sees me and signals for me to wait. It seems like he wants to tell me something but there's also sympathy on his face.

'Why are we here?' asks Romeo once we're standing in the same clearing he had brought me to when I was … not in a fixated state.

'We're here because this might be the last time I'm allowed to see you, since I've been told that I'll be disowned if I see you again.' I snort as he laughs.

'I take it we're not going to abide by those rules; at least I'm not,' he says in a smooth, confident voice.

'She'll issue a restraining order; it won't look good on your college CV,' I warn him.

He chuckles. 'And what will she say? That I took care of you when she couldn't even try? I don't think any court would take her case.'

I smile a bit and then sigh. 'I sometimes wish we were dreams.'

'Why?' he asks innocently.

'Then we could wake up and try again without failure hanging on to our every step.'

'You prefer deception over reality?'

'Yes,' I say and he makes a face. 'Not everyone loves honesty as much as you do. I'd rather have gone my whole life thinking that my dad left us rather than died.'

'But you'd hate him then,' Romeo points out.

'That's better than hating myself,' I say selfishly.

'You're not a very nice person,' he says, wrinkling his nose.

'No one's nice, Romeo, everyone's got some darkness.'

'I know that, but I'm just saying. I also think that if you had the chance to do good, you'd refuse.'

'No,' I say but the 'no' sounds flimsy to me.

'Sometimes people can change but they choose not to,' he says and I sigh at his poetic aspirations.

'Why do you do that?'

'What?'

'The quote thing. I know you make it up, don't act like you don't,' I say suspiciously.

He looks deeply into my eyes and says something that warms my heart to the core. 'I'm just trying to create a memory.'

I decide to share something with him and it doesn't feel sickly sweet or irritating. I used to hate it when people talked about their problems with someone else. *Keep it inside,* I used to think, *don't let them know.* 'That day when we were going for the concert, I thought I was going to create a memory. That's all I've ever wanted to do. And I did create a memory. A bad memory, but still a memory.' He yawns but I know he's paying attention. If he'd tried to stifle that yawn I'd know he wasn't listening. 'How's your mother?' I ask, changing the topic. I immediately see that that wasn't wise. He'd told me his mom was crazy but wasn't in an asylum.

'I don't know. Oliver's parents are my legal guardians.'

'But you'd never seen Oliver before?' I press because I find this interesting. At least something not boring is happening in my life.

'No, just in pictures.'

Then we refrain from talking because the sun has just disappeared and clouds have come out, making the weather chillier and darker. No one wants to spoil the beautiful moment that has taken over the core of the forest. But finally, one of us must be the voice of reason. That's Romeo. 'Juliet, we can't always stay out here in the woods. Teachers are beginning to wonder who the strange boy called Romeo is. I mean, it's fine for you, they're used to you, but I need to study.'

His allegations start to piss me off. 'What do you mean? Are you saying I'm the reason you might fail your exams? Also, my father's death doesn't mean I can skip school!'

He gets up and says to me crossly, 'I'm not accusing you of anything. I'm just saying we can't go to the woods every day!'

I stare at him in complete and utter disbelief. 'Am I forcing you to come here?'

He looks frustrated. 'It's not that. I'm just saying, unlike you, some of us wish to live normal lives. We don't go fishing for trouble and we don't make everything about us. I know you have no motive in life or things that you want to do, but I have a lot of ambitions. I want to be a musician, a poet, a writer or a lawyer … the sky is the limit. Harvard or Stanford would be great options, but I can't get in unless I do well here. So, if you basically want to forget all about having a good life, then stay out in the woods, but if you want to change…'

'So you're saying I cannot get into college,' I say, interrupting him. 'I don't want to go through all of this school, college, work. What's the point? Like, really? Hurray, you studied for fourteen years then another four in college and then you work till you die. It's all so artificial, there's no point to any of it. We have no purpose; we're not working towards anything. We're empty, meaningless. So, let me present you with a great question. And I can bet my life on the fact that you won't have an answer instantly.' I pause. 'What is life?'

His eyebrows knit together and dip to his nose while he thinks. Finally, he whispers to me, '*He drew a circle that shut me out, heretic, rebel, a thing to flout. But love and I had the wit to win, we drew a circle that took him in.'*

I think for a moment because I know those lines: Edwin Markham's. 'That's not fair. You copied someone,' I complain.

'Fine,' he says gently. 'Life is love.'

I stare at him strangely for a second — that's a legit answer but a bit disappointing. Love is a foreign concept to me. I consider love to be the worst mistake made by mankind. Still, to people like him, it's a good answer. 'That's good, I guess,' I say offhandedly.

'So, since you bet your life on it ... I guess you need to be killed,' he jokes.

I look at him sadly. 'You can't kill what is already dead,' I whisper and I'm gone.

I can't let him see the tears I feel build up. I've been waiting for them for so long that when they come they feel pleasant. But they never actually come out of my eyes. I rush out of the forest, not knowing where to go. I can't go home because ... so I trudge all the way to school. It's only one, so lunch must have just started and I haven't eaten in a very long time. I usually skip dinner, I hate Ming-Su.

I walk down the familiar dull white halls and pass my boring classes. The students have all lined up in the lunch hall and distorted chatter can be heard. I notice Oliver sitting with a bunch of kids who look a lot like him. See, I usually eat somewhere near the old, burnt-down lunch hall so I don't have a regular lunch table. I go to join his table and all his friends ignore me. Actually, everyone in the lunch hall seems to be ignoring me in the best way. Some give me sad smiles or sympathetic nods and go back to eating the mush assembled on their plates. Some whisper, 'I thought she wouldn't come.' Or, 'Why is she here? Hasn't she cried at all?' But none of them look shocked; I'm known for doing outrageous things. I look around for Romeo but can't see him – so much for moving on with our futures.

'Hey, Oliver,' I say and hunch over to eat my sandwich. He looks at me and fixes his horn-rimmed glasses. He shouldn't be surprised; I always come at odd times and leave whenever I want. But this time, his face shows clear concern. Oh, right, my dad died. 'I'm fine,' I say before he can ask. His glasses seem to be a bit misty and I see that he's been crying. 'Hey,' I say gently, 'I'm fine, really. He was never around anyway. No need to be sorry for me or anything, just be normal.'

He gives me a gloomy smile and says, 'It's not just that. Marsha...'

My improved mood immediately disappears. 'What's happened to Marsha?'

'She's no more,' he says nervously. 'Well,' he adds, adjusting his glasses again, 'there are two hundred and fifty harmful chemicals in tobacco smoke and, well, she never stops with the cigarettes. So, she digested arsenic, benzene, cadmium, vinyl, nicotine...'

'Cancer,' I say, shaking my head. I always saw all that smoke but I never told her to stop. There had been signs but none of us had bothered enough to notice. All that coughing and wheezing...

'Where is she?'

'Millington Hospital.' Oliver watches me with a sad expression, thinking, *She's finally lost it.*

Well, buddy, I lost it long ago. And I can't help but walk away. It feels exactly like the time when the lunch hall was burning. I can almost hear my friend call out to me. The fire, the flames are so vivid…

I am at the hospital but I don't ask about Marsha. Instead, I get my dad's suitcase from them. It's not that big and is easy to carry. Then I run out of the hospital on to the road. I need to clear my head; everything is so clouded! I need to … I need to…

A car whizzes by me and I dodge it by a millimetre. 'Help!' I yell but no one hears me because it's all in my head. *All in my head.* My head, where the real monsters live. If I could, I would remove my mind, I don't care if I become a vegetable. At least I wouldn't be so disastrous. I lug the suitcase all the way to the forest; the amount of exercise is marvellous. When I get into the familiar clearing, I see Romeo is still lying there. I drop the suitcase before him. A sense of dread creeps up, I'm so tired, so tired … I collapse on the ground.

When I get up, everything is fuzzy and I have a terrible headache. There's this pang in the back of my head but I cannot feel any bruises. I rub it, moaning a bit as I do so. My eyes adjust and I see that I'm in the woods. Faint light filters in from the gaps in the canopy. A very tired Romeo is lying down next to me. His face looks worn and he seems to be resting peacefully.

That's when all the recent events hit me hard, like when you rip off a Band-Aid. 'Romeo,' I say and he is up at once.

'You're okay now? You were crying yesterday.'

I wince. Why did I cry? I didn't have permission to do that. 'That's a one-time thing,' I warn him and he chuckles lightly. 'So aren't you going to school?' I ask somewhat bitterly.

He sighs and apologizes for saying anything about that. But as he continuously keeps glancing behind, I understand that he wants to go back.

'Go to school,' I tell him. He ignores my suggestion. 'Yesterday you said ... something about indirectly killing someone.' Dread creeps up on me again, did I tell him?

'Did you bully someone or...?' he asks, getting completely the wrong idea.

I start to say no, but bite my lip along the way. 'Yeah, old memories.'

He smiles wistfully. 'Still want memories?'

I smile but I'm not able to look into his eyes.

His voice turns serious. 'How did you get over it so easily?'

I look up at him and ask, 'What?'

'Your dad's death and Marsha's death,' he says, not beating around the bush.

'Oh,' I say, blushing. *If only he knew.* 'I just don't do emotions, I guess.'

He lays himself down on the soft green grass, 'Tell me.'

'I just did!'

'You and I both don't believe that. How did you get over it so fast? And your mom threatening you? How are you so strong?'

'Trust me, I'm not strong. I guess I find other ways to face sorrow.'

'I wonder what it would be like to be you...' he says, thinking aloud. I sense that he doesn't know he just spoke out loud so I don't answer. 'Well?' he says after a long moment of silence.

I realize he was asking me a question. 'It would probably be the worst thing in the world. It's not fun being me. Sometimes I just wish that ... that I could leave this body, this life behind and start afresh. Everyone deserves a second chance,' I say firmly and he nods.

'Yeah, but you can't remove every memory you ever had. You can't forget everything. You can try, but some people would have made a huge difference and you can't change that.'

'Maybe ... but I just want to leave. I want to pick up everything and leave forever. I don't want to live anywhere for too long, I want to move around. But the problem is, humans have explored every country in the world, there's no unknown left for us. I just ... I can't face this any more. *I need to break out of the system.*'

He smiles dreamily. 'Yeah, but Harvard, Stanford, so much potential...'

I try my hardest not to snort. Those are his dreams? To go do what everyone has gone and done? Do what's being done by at least one billion people? 'I don't want to die, but I don't want to live in this world,' I say to him and he frowns.

'Where would you go?'

Somewhere no one has ever been before and I'd live in solitude. Because when you're alone, no one can judge you and you can be yourself in your secret place. 'My sanctuary,' I say, answering his question, and he refrains from asking where or what that is. The truth is, I don't know either, but I want to find out.

'We'll need to go to class tomorrow,' he says, changing the topic.

'You mean *you* will need to go,' I correct him.

'No, both of us are going to study,' he says obstinately.

'I don't like to study and I hate school.'

He makes a face. 'Big deal, everyone hates school.'

'But my dad and my friend just died,' I say, excusing myself politely.

'Most people won't use death as their own personal excuse but you, you wear it on your head like a crown.' He looks disgusted.

'Do you think I like it that my friend and my dad are dead? I just don't see the point in acting like death doesn't happen. It does, do you want more proof?' I say forcefully. He moves back and I find it's funny to taunt him. 'Death, death, death, death, death,' I say and watch his face grow more and more black.

'Stop it!' he yells and crouches down.

'Why?' I say, still taunting him.

He covers his face with his hands. 'No reason.'

After staying in the woods for a while longer, breathing in the fresh, clean air, I go home because school isn't where I want to be. The door isn't open; it's evident Mom's home. I already know what I'm going to do. Sneak in behind her and make a dash for my room. But my plans are foiled as some tiny bimbo opens the door. She looks about twelve and is the prettiest creature I've ever seen. She has big, wide eyes, very different from my slanted feline ones. Her cheeks are rose red, the opposite of my droopy pale cheeks. She's wearing a shirt that says *I Love My Mum*, compared to my shirt that says … well, I don't know what it says because it's covered in dirt and grass and *evil*.

'Hey,' she says and her voice has sugar in it.

I almost gag but then my mom appears behind her. Her shirt says: *I Love My Daughter*. I almost throw up. 'Juliet,' she says and proudly points to the little beauty. 'This is my new daughter. She's everything I wanted in a daughter and more. Also, she doesn't throw away opportunities. Her name is Elle. A beautiful name, don't you think?' she asks me abstractedly.

'It's wonderful,' I say blandly.

'She's my true daughter,' my mom (should I even call her that?) continues. 'She is a blessing and she's helped me so much already. And look at her thick hair, such a nice change from your dark, mangy curls.'

I nod. Of course she has a new daughter. When you're sad you always adopt, right?

'Elle, be a darling and get me some water, please,' says Mom kindly.

Elle sashays towards the kitchen. 'Mom, what the hell did you just do?' I ask.

'What do you mean, Juliet? Is it wrong to adopt a perfectly amazing girl who you couldn't be even in your dreams?' she asks matter-of-factly. Her insult might have hurt (it does a bit) if she'd delivered it like an insult. Her tone is far-off, distant and loose, sort of like how Disney princesses talk.

'No, it's perfectly okay,' I tell her and she smiles happily, but there's something else in her smile that I can't quite identify.

'Oh, by the way, Elle's going to share your room,' she calls out as I run to my room.

I shut the door, breathing hard. My room, *my room,* that's my private space. I take out my black marker and write *unworthy, replaced, different, unrequited* on my arms and thighs but within the boundaries. Always within the boundaries. I quickly hide the marker and go to the shower. The hot water feels soothing as it runs downs my back, flowing like a waterfall. I change into something comfortable and then decide against it. I decide to wear the long purple frock my mother had once bought for me. It looks rough and scratchy and it doesn't quite fit. 'It's better than nothing,' I mutter and come out of my room. Elle and my mom are laughing at something Elle said. I feel a pang of jealousy, as I could never get my mom to even smile.

'Hey,' I say nervously, smoothing my gown.

'Are we having dinner with the queen?' jokes Elle, trying to make my mother laugh again.

But my mother's lips don't quiver with laughter; instead, they quiver with rage. 'What are you doing in that?' she asks, her voice threateningly thin.

'I thought you'd like it,' I mumble.

'I don't. What do you think you're getting at, dressing up like that inside the house? You couldn't be bothered to run a brush through that mane of yours when we used to go out.'

'I'm just trying on something different! You don't have to yell at me for it!'

'Give that dress to Elle this instant. She's only twelve and yet it will look better on her than you. Don't you ever waste my money again!'

'I just did something nice for you!'

She sneers. 'Something nice for me? When have you ever wanted to do something nice for me? You ditched me the moment your father died.'

'I needed my space. I can't hold your hand through everything!'

'And yet you continue to live here?'

'I'm still a minor, I'm not allowed to leave home. Believe me, if it wasn't illegal, I'd have done it years ago!'

Elle nervously cuts into our yelling voices, her voice tiny and small compared to our bellowing screams. 'Please don't fight.'

Mom looks at her delicately and holds her pale hand. 'I'm so sorry you had to see Juliet like that … Juliet can be a bit of a devil,' she says, glaring at me.

I don't know what to say, so I shamefully leave the room and enter my own. Then I let out a loud groan and rip up the dress. The pieces fall to the floor soundlessly, very different from the clang I was expecting. 'You idiot!' I scream to no one in particular.

Then I rush out and, in my rage, I slap my mom. She looks shocked at my action, which seems to hurt her more than the actual slap.

Elle gasps and weeps. 'How could you hurt our mother?' she asks me and moves away, afraid I might turn on her too.

The words 'our mother' irritate me and I fire up. 'She's not our mother, she's *my* mother,' I point out and she cowers.

Mom's face turns crimson and she bellows into my ear, 'No, I'm not your mother, you never let me be. Now I'm Elle's and only Elle's mother.'

Her statement calms me down a bit. *Is she disowning me?*

'Yes, I am,' she says and I realize I asked that out loud.

'You can't, it's not legal,' I say doubtfully.

She thinks for a second before coming up with a solution. 'I'll just say you ran away because you have to leave now,' she says forcefully. When I don't move, she rises to her full height. 'Do you need some help?' she asks, her voice filled with venom.

Tears begin to flow from Elle's eyes. She doesn't seem particularly mean, but she doesn't seem very nice either. She sort of just stands there, crying at the right parts but otherwise completely invisible.

'I need a place to stay!' I object.

'Don't you have *friends?*' she asks, watching my face. 'Of course not, who'd want to be friends with a heartless bitch like you?'

This is when I question the universe again. How did my sweet, gentle and annoying mother become such an A-class brat? When did she change? What happened? 'Well, everyone likes Ming-Su and I hate Ming-Su,' I say stupidly without thinking. My mother assumes I'm talking about a person.

'Maybe this Ming-Su actually possesses a heart.'

I laugh. 'Ming-Su is a noodle place. You know I hate Ming-Su and yet you always bring me noodles from there!' I complain. Why am I talking about noodles at a time like this?

'I never brought you Ming-Su. I don't even know what that is,' she says and points to the fridge, which I run to.

I open the door, getting slightly refreshed by the cool inside. Sure enough, there are no Ming-Su boxes. Only Noodle Bar boxes. 'Sorry,' I mutter, almost inaudibly. But she hears and gives a macabre laugh.

'You're really stupid, unlike my precious princess, Elle!' she says and smiles maliciously. As if hurting me is the best feeling in the world. '*Go!*' she yells.

'*Fine!*' I yell back. 'You're useless anyway, Mom, or should I just call you Random Lady!' Then I run to my room and hazily pack my bag. I put in completely useless things. The only good thing I put in is a toothbrush. But I don't forget my money because that's the only wealth I have now. Random Lady will probably cut me out of her will, if I have ever been in it. Elle, dear Elle, will surely get my share by batting her long, black eyelashes and widening her big, round eyes. Sometimes I wish everyone was blind so you could judge a person by their behaviour and not their face.

Once I come out of my room, Random Lady pretends I'm not even there. 'You are my true daughter, Elle,' she murmurs to the other girl, gently caressing her soft hair. Elle looks slightly frightened to see me; she blinks and watches me bang the door in rage.

The air is cold and misty, just like it was a few days ago. I'm freezing because all I'm wearing is a thin shirt and shorts. The roads and pavements are slippery, making it easy to slide and fall. Droplets hang off trees and I wonder if it rained. Cars pass by and they zoom ahead, not bothering to notice an ordinary girl. I walk with no definite direction, pass countless houses. Basically, I am speed but not velocity. The sodium-powered lamps switch on just as my watch reads eight and I'm starving for dinner. I don't even have that much money on me so a hotel is not an option. And I don't have any friends – wait, that's not true – Romeo! Of course, he might not want to take me in given that I fought with him, but would he refuse someone asking for shelter? And he lives with Oliver, who'd be sure to let me in. At least for this one night, this badly-prepped-for for, explosive night ... The thought of Elle sleeping in my bed, going through my things, my black marker. No, not my marker. That marker is my lifeline and I couldn't possibly live without it. I suddenly have a certain hunger to ink words on my skin right then. If I don't, they might fade away and take me with them. The words I ink in are confirmation that I'm still here and have not gone to an extraordinary beyond. Besides, the smooth and soft tip of the marker feels good and its press on my skin feels like home. Not Random Lady's home but a true home. A place to reside and live in, completely at peace with yourself – that's home. The suitcase! What happened to the suitcase? How could I have been so careless as to lose that? My dad's final present to me and I didn't care for its worth. I walk on and on before noticing the sign that points towards Oliver's house. But Oliver's mom might not like to see me, and she'd probably call my mom and ask her to come pick me up. And then there'd be a lot of drama and I hate drama.

When I reach Oliver's well-maintained and neat house, I slow down. I take a chance by going to the side of the house where the curtains are parted. Aunty is sitting on the couch and facing the television. I can't make out but it looks like she's watching the news. Oliver is sitting next to her. His dad (who doesn't know me) is sitting on the dining table and adjusting the mats and the food. 'Romeo!' he calls, once he's done. 'It's dinner time!' A sound of thumping is heard coming down the stairs and Romeo is sitting next to the head of the table. Oliver and his mom join and they engage in polite conversation. Oliver's eyes dart to the side and I'm afraid he might see me, so I duck. His eyes glaze over and he obviously doesn't know that someone is watching him and his family eat. The tone and atmosphere of the conversation gets a bit harsher as they start talking about me, and I instantly tune in, trying my hardest to make out the words.

'I really don't like you spending time with that wild girl, Juliet,' Aunty says, her lips at their thinnest. 'She spoiled Oliver and now she'll ruin you too. Romeo, you used to study so hard, your mom used to say, and now look at your grades.' She frowns. 'Oh, right, they're non-existent because you didn't sit for a single test!'

Romeo swallows his food before looking her straight in the eye. 'That's not Juliet's fault, and I just arrived here, please allow me some time to adjust.'

'That can be given but can it be maintained?' Oliver's dad says cleverly.

'Listen, I'll try my hardest, okay? Juliet's father and one of her friends just died. I think she's permitted some grieving time,' Romeo says, agitated by their clear disapproval of me.

'Of course she does, but her mom is such a nice person … What happened to Juliet? How did she become like this?'

The rest of their dinner continues in silence as my name has brought some shame to the table. They finish eating and go their separate ways. I still don't know whether to seek shelter here or go to the police. Maybe I should just go home and Mom will come to me and apologize and say it was all an act. Elle will go back to wherever she came from and the earth will spin in slow-mo again. Also, I desperately need to get my marker back since my skin is itching for it. I notice the light go on in a room upstairs and can make out Romeo's profile and it makes me smile. A portion of the house juts out and makes it easy to climb up to the window. It's a classic movie scene, except getting on to the part that juts out is almost impossible. Almost. I somehow grab the ledge and haul myself up. Then I climb on to Romeo's window but find it shut. I knock but not too loud. I can see Romeo playing his guitar but can't hear the notes. I bang against the glass, wishing I had a diamond-tip knife to cut through it. He looks up, obviously disturbed. When he sees it's me, he gives me an exasperated look. He opens the window and closes his door so no one will see me.

'What are you doing here?' he asks, irritated but concerned.

'I need a place to crash tonight…' I say and wait for him to offer his bed. 'Why?' he asks suspiciously.

'My…' I begin, not knowing what to say next, '… mom disowned me so I don't have a place to stay any more.'

His expression holds disbelief. 'Come on, Juliet, I thought you could lie better than that. For starters, it's illegal to disown a minor.'

'I know, but she'll make up some story, and anyway she has a new daughter, Elle,' I say, spitting out the name with such hatred that he starts to believe me.

'Fine, you can stay here as long as you want, but we'll need to get you a new place because … I don't think Oliver's mom likes you.'

'I know, I heard.'

He smiles but only after seeing me smile. 'We need to get you a place to stay. So, do you have any other friends except Oliver?'

I look away, as this is an uncomfortable topic. 'I don't really like humans.'

'I'm not human?'

'No,' I say and for some reason he grins.

'Do you want to be adopted? But I don't think anyone will adopt you, you're way too old,' he says and switches on his computer. 'Or you can just go home.'

'I can't, she doesn't want me to go home and I can't live there, she might murder me some day and then…'

'We could find some abandoned house for you and I can bring you food and stuff,' he says. 'That's illegal, though.'

I smile, an idea coming to my mind. 'It's not illegal to go to school. I could just stay in the lunch hall. No one even goes there any more.'

He chuckles. 'It's an idea but we need to go further than that. We have to sue,' he says and gives a maniacal grin.

'Sue my mom?' I say coherently.

'Who else? She forced you out on to the streets without any means. She abandoned a minor for whom she is responsible, so she should be put into jail,' he says simply.

Some people might shy away from putting their moms in jail, but not me. 'We need a lawyer,' I say.

He thinks for a moment and then types something into Google search. A million results pop up and he goes to the first one. 'This one gives an address for a lawyer who fights for minors but only if they have evidence. He's old and charitable, so he does it for free.'

I cross my arms. 'She threw me on the street. That's evidence enough.'

'Yeah, but it might not work and I think you should just talk to her. If not face to face, then at least on the phone. Stay here tonight and then apologize tomorrow,' he suggests.

'Why should I apologize for something she did?' I ask bitterly.

'We can't sue her; we don't have enough of a case. And do you want a place to live or not?' he asks me, his tone serious.

'I just want to be okay,' I say in a whiny voice.

He gently puts me in his bed and pulls the cover up. 'I'm not going to force you to do anything. But calling your mom will make things okay. All she wants is to be a mother to you, so be her daughter.'

'Play the song you were playing,' I order tiredly. I close my eyes as he begins to play a soft tune, which sends me back to memories of my father.

When I was a little girl, my dad and I would look at clouds and wonder what shapes they were. We never said things like *it's so pretty* or *so big*. No, we would stare until we could discern exactly what it was. If it was a big one, then it would be a bear or a lion. I remember asking him what life is. He had thought for a second and then looked at me softly. Eyes full of fatherly care, he'd whispered, 'Life is discovering what you never knew.' I had smiled at him and my mom had entered the scene. She was wearing a blue dress with yellow flowers and her hair looked perfect. She'd brought us juice. For some reason my mother couldn't stop bringing us juice or food or sunscreen. She kept smothering us with care and, god, was it suffocating! Still, being the nice person I was, I asked her what life is. She smiled but she didn't like my curious nature. She

wiped my face and scolded my dad for staying out in the sun.
'Life is life, dear,' she said. She was a great caregiver but that's
all she was. After a few years, she stopped caring for a while.
She just disappeared; she gave me food and everything but she
stopped smothering me. This was before Dad died and once
he died, she became her needy self again. And then she kicked
me out because I didn't stay with her. She's a bomb slowly
ticking its life away…

I wake up, remembering last night's events. I'm still not sure
whether to return home. A sudden headache seizes my temples
and I feel woozy and everything spins.

'Hide!' hisses Romeo, who's already dressed. He's standing
near the door, peeking through the keyhole. I quickly rush to the
bathroom and lock myself in, but I don't see Romeo's reaction.
The bathroom is surprisingly clean and a sweet lavender smell
wafts around. I hear Aunty come in and she's followed by
Oliver, from the sound of it.

'Romeo, you have to go to school today. Oliver will make
sure you do … Now, quickly get ready and please don't talk
to that girl again.' She finds it shameful to even say my name!
I unlock the door once I hear her leave and find Romeo and
Oliver talking. Oliver shrieks but not very loudly, so no one
except Romeo and I hear.

'What are you doing here?' he squeals. 'Mom isn't going to
be happy to see you here, no offence.'

'Mom isn't going to know,' Romeo tells him threateningly.

Oliver crouches down, obviously afraid.

'Don't scare him!' I scold. 'We trust you, Oliver.'

'The phone call, now!' says Romeo, thrusting his phone towards me.

I make up my mind to beg for forgiveness. However cowardly it is, I don't want to live in the lunch hall and sue my mom for something so bizarre. I dial her number and she picks up on the second ring. Her voice is as feathery light as I remember but there is a hard bottom to it.

'Hello?' she says and there is the sound of Elle laughing in the background.

'Hey, Mom,' I say and wait for her to erupt. When she doesn't, I rush into my apology. Romeo ushers Oliver out of the room and I mouth a thank-you to him. 'Listen, I'm really sorry for leaving you alone that day at the hospital. I'm sorry for yelling at you and not being your daughter.'

I can almost hear her smile at the other end. 'I'm sorry for yelling at you too. I think we both said things we didn't mean. And I hadn't been caring for you as much as I should have, but now I'm going to make up for it. Elle will be your new sister and she'll have her own room. Just come back, darling,' she coos and I flash a fake grin at Romeo.

'I'm going back, she's sorry too,' I say, once I've put down the phone.

Romeo doesn't smile because he notices my unease. 'You're fine going back, right?' I smile but it doesn't reach my eyes. 'I'm fine,' I say and sneak out the way I had come in.

No one notices me and I walk the lonely way back to my house. I fear that my meeting with Mom will be awkward. But it's not. She and Elle are standing on the porch and there's a huge banner which reads *We're Sorry*. I smile in spite of myself. Mom gives me a hug and I can smell her lemony scent. Elle looks perfect as usual, but Mom has eyes for me and only me.

'You must be hungry, I ordered pizza,' she says and Elle follows us inside.

Once we're seated, we have a nice breakfast. It's the first time in years that we're sitting as a family and having a meal together. We make small talk, but Mom doesn't say a thing about school. She fusses over me and I sort of enjoy it. She used to do this a lot before she went into her weird period of solitary living. She combs my hair and plaits it. She gives me plenty of drinks and snacks that I actually like. For once in my life, I feel like I might have a happy ending. We go through the day together and Mom can't leave me alone, but I don't mind. At around three in the afternoon, we decide to have another meal and my mom touches my face lightly. I don't like it when anyone touches my face, but I permit Mom to and that pleases her greatly.

'You're the picture of health,' she murmurs after inspection.

I don't know whether I'm imagining it but I think I hear a frown in her voice.

'Thank you?' I ask, raising my eyebrow.

She looks provoked for a second before giving me a dazzling smile.

'I have a tasty drink for you.'

I smile wearily – I'm getting tired of her drinks.

She brings me a tall glass filled with a red liquid. 'Drink this,' she says with a certain control to her voice. I finish it in a minute. It tastes good, so good that I want more. Even my headache seems to disappear. I smile widely and grin at her and she smiles back. 'Elle likes it too.'

I smile happily and flounce around. What should I do now? Maybe draw? Yes, I like drawing and colouring. I'll draw a cherry because cherries are red and I like red ... I go around the house cheerfully for about an hour before collapsing in the living room.

When I wake up, my head hurts without any specific cause. 'Ow!' I let out. There's a searing pain in my head and it keeps getting stronger. It throbs so hard and it doesn't stop stinging. Even though it hurts so much, I don't cry. I cannot cry, I cannot show weakness ... 'Mom!' I yell, but I'm still not crying.

My mother appears by my side in a second and she holds me up. 'It's going to be okay, dear. My baby, it won't hurt once Mommy stops it,' she says and drags me to her room.

I barely take in my surroundings because I'm shivering with the pain. 'Mom!' I say impatiently but I don't cry. I cannot allow myself to cry. She makes me lie down on her big bed. Thin rays of sun appear through gaps in the curtain. I can see her wardrobe in one corner and there's the furnished wall which was done with so much care ... and then there's nothing. Just a dark oblivion which sends fear through my body, but I don't cry. All this pain cannot match up to the humiliation I'd feel if I cry. The last thing I see before completely losing myself is my

Mom's pale, plastic face. Her big, red lips are the last thing I see before closing my eyes.

When I open my eyes, I feel a lot better than how I had felt. 'Mom?' I ask wearily. I see glossy curls and Elle comes closer to me and her eyes are open wide. She looks terrified. 'I'm okay,' I say and get up. And I do feel fine, I feel normal, not strong but not weak either. She comes closer to me and I see Mom walking in.

'You're awake,' she says happily. 'You'll be fine, don't worry. Mommy took good care of you.'

'No doubt, at least I can stand up now,' I say stoically.

She puts an arm around me and takes me to my old room and takes Elle somewhere with her. 'Thanks, Mom,' I say sincerely before she closes the door. She doesn't say anything but I see her smile. Then I rummage through my drawers before finding my most prized possession. I pull up my sticky shirt and write *sick, careful, hungry, okay, unable* on my hand. I write more and more, relishing the touch of the pen. I worry about my psychological state and then I don't worry. Crazy people don't know they're crazy. I slowly rest my head on the pillow. It's only eight but I feel sleepy.

The next few weeks pass easily and I stay carefree. I don't fall ill like that again and I go through Mom's continuous and never-ending care. She is my mother after all, and if she doesn't take care of me, then who will? Elle doesn't speak to me much except to ask for the time or to ask where Mom is. I think she's scared of me.

I attend school once in a while, otherwise I just rest in the woods. Oliver doesn't mention my 'visit' to his house and he doesn't comment on Marsha's death. I simply put her in the back of my head with my friend who died in the fire. Romeo goes to school and sits for every test but sometimes we go to the woods together. We don't talk much; the silence speaks for us in the woods. I sit through the tests too, and do okay for someone who doesn't go for a single lesson. The thing is, I don't care about my future. I don't want to have the 'normal' future everyone else has. Sometimes I wonder if I even want a future.

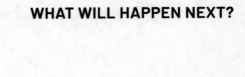

WHAT WILL HAPPEN NEXT?

My mother had been so busy setting up the table with the pink swirly tablecloths we'd bought last week and placing candles in the centre of the table that she didn't hear the doorbell ring. She'd taken three hours to get ready, wiping on and off different shades of red lipstick until she finally settled on one that looked to me like the colour of rust. In her flouncy cream dress with frills tied with ribbons on the ends, she looked like a village girl going to school in the big city.

No matter how hard she tried, my mother always looked to me like a child.

When I opened the door and let my father in, I started to feel more than a little nauseous because it had been three years since I'd last seen him, but his deodorant still smelt the same. The crisp smell of menthol and mint.

My father settled down on the dining chair and rested his hands very carefully on the table, so as to not disturb the arrangement my mother had made with the knife and the fork and the plate. He took out a cigarette and lighter and, in an instant, grey ash was falling on the floor again, the same grey ash I had once pretended was fairy dust.

'Hi,' my mother said, once she stepped out of the kitchen. She smiled at him lasciviously and I felt like laughing because it was almost as if she was expecting him to give her the red lollipops he used to give me when I was a child.

'It's good to see you, been a long time.' He leaned forward a bit, as if he was thinking of embracing her, but then decided against it at the last minute and took a long puff of his cigarette instead. 'How've you been, my girl?' Smoke danced out of his mouth. He looked at me. 'My two girls.'

'Just give us a sec, I need to get the lamb.' My mother waved at me and I followed her into the kitchen. It really was a horrible kitchen. Every time I looked at it, I found it hard to believe I'd been living here for ten years. There were Winnie the Pooh and Hannah Montana stickers all over the fridge because neither my mother nor I had the patience to tear them off. Then there was that sickly black exhaust vent that seemed almost malicious to me, the whirring sound it made when my mother cooked became a menacing growl. We only used the ancient cooking stove below it on special occasions because otherwise the countertop on which it rested would become too hot and small holes like pinpricks would start to form.

'Get the lamb out of the oven, put rosemary and thyme on top,' my mother told me.

It was very difficult for me to take my mother seriously when she tried commanding me. Her voice turned into this nasally high-pitched sound, and it sounded like a bell was tinkling each time she spoke.

'Put some pepper too.' *Ting.*

'I already put salt.' *Ting.*

'Take the potatoes out.' *Ting.*

By the time I took the potatoes and the lamb out to the table in transparent casserole dishes whose ugly yellow covers my mother had thrown to the back of a cupboard somewhere, my father was already on his third cigarette. He had placed the butts of the earlier two on the table neatly, one in line with the other. I couldn't tell if he thought he was being considerate.

'Come here, lovely.' He didn't say it in a smiling sort of way. He said it in the way a train conductor might ask for your ticket.

That was the thing with my father; you never knew what was coming next.

'Come on, give your father a hug. It's been ages since I've seen you, ages. Last I saw you, we were talking about buying you an island.'

If this was a movie, I thought, I would already be in his arms.

He laughed before sucking on his cigarette again. 'Say, your mother doesn't happen to have any wine, does she? I wouldn't ask normally, but it was a long flight getting here, you know. Come on.'

As my mother entered the room with a big, bright, stiff smile on her face, I opened the small liquor cabinet we had in the corner of the room. I don't even know why we had it. My mother only drank in company (which neither of us had much of) and it was hardly for me, although I did spend a lot of afternoons seated in front of it, trying out the different bottles while my mother was at work. Through trial and error, and a lot of evenings spent clutching my stomach and holding my breath as I poured the liquor in, I found my favourite. Whisky. Gave me a quick rush to the head and filled me with a sort of warmth in my stomach. This was how I spent my days in the summer: I sat on the floor, raiding my mother's booze and watching the afternoon sun glower down at me. Sometimes I would make plans to go out to a nearby mall, or to a restaurant with a friend who had sent me the obligatory *I miss you* message because it was summer and we had to pretend to at least somewhat like each other. But every time it got closer to the date, the thought of *actually* meeting someone would scare me, make me so restless that I couldn't sleep, and I spent hours at night staring at the window opposite my bed.

My father called out for me loudly as if I wasn't just two feet away from him. 'What's the idea, going to take another eternity or what?'

I clutched the bottle of red wine in my hand, my thoughts in a flurry as I hoped my mother wouldn't notice that almost two-thirds of it was gone, even though she hadn't had any of it since May when she'd hosted her book club meeting. (They'd discussed *House of Mirth*, and my mother had said, 'Edith really gets to the troubles of the times, doesn't she?').

I handed the wine to my father and took my seat in between my mother, who was at one end of the table, and my father, who was at the other end. It wasn't a long table; it was stumpy and square and had cracks and scratches all over it. There was a portion where I had carved my name into the wood that I hadn't noticed in a while, mostly because the initial M in my name looked like four unrelated scratches that were too close together.

'Good girl,' my father said to me and peered at my mother, who was cutting her steak into halves and then into quarters. She always did this. She always played with her food. She never ate anything.

'So, Anne, tell me, how are you?' My father suddenly looked very pleased with himself – his thick black eyebrows relaxed and his face settled into a softer shape. It always surprised me how fast my father could seem so calm, so at ease. It shouldn't have, but it did. 'How's work?'

'It's all right, you know. We have our good days, we have our bad. I've been promoted to sales manager now. It comes with an increase in salary. I was surprised when they offered it to me, I really was – I've never seen myself as any kind of a leader, you know, never have.'

'Well, I always told you, you're going to be someone great. Next president or something.'

My mother beamed and shook her head but she was laughing. The ringlets she had pinned back on her head came askew and made her look even more demure. I felt sort of sorry for her right then. It wasn't that I liked her very much, nothing like that; in fact, sometimes I wondered how someone could be so proud of their ignorance like her, but right then I felt bad for her in the way you might feel bad for the slow kid getting teased in school. She didn't even realize she was being patronized.

'I think you should try, Anne. I know I've never said it before, but you should. Salesgirl turned mayor. One of the people, fighting for the people. Something clever like that.' My father nudged me and took out another cigarette. 'You could make posters for your mom.'

My mother threw her head back and howled with laughter. Her body was almost convulsing. I hadn't seen her this energetic in days. 'You must think I love you because you flatter me. Also, sales manager now, no longer salesgirl.'

'You're important now, Anne, I see that. Real important. You're a big girl now. Don't need me any more.'

I could feel the back of my neck getting hot and I was starting to feel pretty angry at my father. Not at how he was talking down to my mother, but really at how he was pretending he was someone to talk up to. This kind of thing bothered me, this unsaid agreement of who is being talked up to and who is being talked down to and how the one being talked down to never has a say.

'Of course I need you. You're welcome to come back now, you know that. Anytime you'd like. She can take the couch or I can, and you can sleep here. It creaks a little and I know your shoulder hurts, that's why I'm thinking you should take the bed.'

'I'd like to come back.' My father yawned and pulled out another cigarette. It really annoyed me, the way he placed all the butts in a line, not even crushing them, so there were now five cigarette burns on the tablecloth. It wasn't a frighteningly exquisite or a very expensive tablecloth, but it mattered all the same. He was burning it because he didn't care, because he wasn't the one who'd have to clean the tablecloth in our half-broken washing machine tomorrow, because he could get on a plane and forget us and I couldn't. I thought of screaming at my mother, *He's not coming back.* I thought of how her face would crumple if I said it, and the foundation she had put on (costing 800 bucks, which we could have spent on three meals) would fall to the floor in scratchy flakes as the air in her body would be let out and she'd lie on the ground like an inflatable toy I could stomp on.

'But I don't want to get into that now. That's a grown-up discussion I need to have with your mother, if I really do come back.' He turned to me. 'I want to talk about you, how're you doing in school?'

'All right. I'm taking advanced math.'

'What are you doing in math? Pythagoras, hmmm?'

'Dad, tell us about what you've been doing. You've been doing something, haven't you? At the hospital?' I'd like to think my voice sounded very pointed and haughty, like I'd caught him out. Instead, I'd probably sounded as overzealous as those chickens who squeal right before they're slaughtered.

'I don't understand what's wrong with you. I've come here for a nice dinner with you. I think I should be treated with some respect. I provide for that education you're not telling me about.'

'Sorry, Dad. We did Pythagoras four years ago, now we're on to differentiation.'

My father nodded his head violently, as if that would somehow convince me he knew what I was talking about. It wasn't that he didn't know what differentiation was, he probably did; he just didn't know when I was supposed to be taught it.

'Good job! You liked numbers even as a kid. I still remember how you used to do your homework every day after school, and anytime I asked if you wanted to watch some TV, you said not till five because you had planned it all out in your little diary – math from four to five, and then you'd relax till six and then you'd go out to play with your friends and then we'd have dinner. Every day. Once, I asked you if you ever got bored doing the same thing every day. You know what you said?' My father smiled at my mother who giggled. 'You said it's not like anybody ever did anything different anyway. That people did the same thing every day and just tried to convince themselves that they were leading exciting lives. I'm paraphrasing here, obviously, but I think this was what you meant. You were talking about how everyone is afraid of being like everyone, of being normal.'

I couldn't remember ever having done this. But my father was certain I had, and he was beaming at me and he had stopped smoking his cigarettes and his hand was very close to my mother's and I was sure he would put his arm around her and soon we'd be living together again and we'd have dinner together every night and anytime he'd go away on work trips he'd smile when he saw us calling his phone and all of this probably would have happened if it wasn't for the sound that boomed across the room next.

The sound came from upstairs and it made my father scowl and say, 'Goddamn it, we're trying to have a meal.'

My mother's eyes flitted nervously from my father's face to the ceiling and I wondered if she was going to say something, if she even had anything to say. I wondered what she had been like as a child. I wondered how her mother had felt when she realized she had a dud for a child.

The sound came again, louder this time, and it didn't stop. It was like something was falling on the floor of the apartment above us, like somebody was throwing all the furniture around and plates were crashing on to the floor and paintings were slipping off the nails on the walls.

'What is this?' my father said. Beads of sweat laced over his upper lip and the vein in his forehead was throbbing. 'What kind of shithole do you live in, Anne?'

'No, no, this has never happened before. You can't blame me for some unwholesome neighbours. Ask her, has this ever happened before?' My mother glared at me.

'No, I don't think so,' I said. 'Not before, no. There is the occasional ambulance, but other than that, it is always silent.'

'See, don't worry, I've been keeping our daughter safe.'

'It's not her safety I'm worried about.' My father raised his pinkie and pointed it to the ceiling. 'It will affect her manners if she hears people screaming and throwing things all day long.' He gave me a lopsided grin, as if to tell me he was only joking.

Now that he mentioned it, I could hear the screaming. It was hardly discernible amidst the louder and more caustic sounds of furniture being crashed into, but I could hear a few words and two voices, a male and a female. They were shouting at each other and throwing things.

'Should we go upstairs and say something? It's so annoying. You go say something.'

This situation was pretty much perfect for my mother. My father would go up, let out all of his anger and frustration, and when he'd come back down he'd have lost all the energy he had, so he would be forced to adhere to my mother's expectations and wishes. Maybe my mother wasn't the idiot and my father was, maybe they were both idiots, maybe they were geniuses disguising themselves as ordinary people so as to not get sent away to a government agency to be tested.

'Yes.' My father stood up and pushed away his wine glass, which was completely empty now. Drops of wine clung to his lower lip. 'I'll go tell them that we live in a decent society, and in a decent society such people are unwelcome.'

'You should take Mom, they'll respond better to a woman,' I said and stabbed at the overcooked lamb. 'They'll be less likely to hurt you.'

If this had been any another day and my father hadn't been about to go and seek revenge, he would have probably started an argument about the double standards of feminism and the problems men face that are overlooked because women's issues are given more importance. He would have probably looked to my mother for approval and she'd have gently patted his head and said, 'We all have our problems.'

'All right,' my father said. 'Anne, let's go.'

'Are you sure you want to intrude though? It is their business. They need privacy.'

My father snorted. 'Well, they should have thought about privacy a few hundred decibels ago.' He pulled my mother's arm the way you pull a dog by its leash. 'Let's go, Anne, we'll be polite, don't worry.'

My parents came back an hour later, laughing about something to themselves.

'Perfect couple,' my father said and took out another cigarette while my mother stood with her arms on his shoulders. They looked like wax figurines to me, especially because of the way my mother's chest was unmoving, as if she was holding her breath, and the stiff way in which my father was sucking his cigarette.

'Yes, it felt good to get there and sort things out for them,' my mother said.

'We explained to them – listen, this is important for when you have a family of your own.' He addressed me, 'We explained to them that no matter what happens, it is important to talk it out and get everything out of your system. No point holding it in.'

'Your father is right. You should know that your family is the only people you can be free with. Everyone else will judge you,' my mother said.

'Will you be staying with us then?' I asked my father.

He laughed and my mother gained life and sat up straight at the table. 'If anyone wants more potatoes, they're in the kitchen. There isn't much left, so if you want some you should get up now.'

ROMEO AND JULIET - III

'Are you coming?' asks Romeo on the phone. Mom and Elle are chatting in the back so it's hard to hear him.

'One second,' I say and move to the privacy of my room. 'Where?'

'The party. You have to come, it's the event of the year!'

Oh yeah, I forgot to mention, Romeo suddenly became popular. I mean, once he started showing up at school, his looks did it all for him. So Romeo's friends keep coming up in huge numbers. Everyone wants to be his friend and buddy. Every girl in the school is completely taken by him except me.

'No,' I say shortly.

'Come on, Chor will be there!'

'Who the hell is Chor?'

Romeo gives an exasperated sigh. 'The poor guy actually likes you.'

I don't feel anything as I don't even know Chor. 'Well, I'm a perfectly likeable person; besides, he doesn't even know me.'

'He likes your face then, I don't know. Give the guy a chance, he has the courage to *like you*.'

'Why is everyone scared of me?' I ask with a sigh. I'm seriously tired of everyone scurrying out of my way. I'd rather have them make fun of me or plot against me.

'I swear this party will change everything,' Romeo says confidently. I know that won't happen but I want to be treated like a human being.

'Okay,' I say. It's Sunday morning so I have quite a few hours before the party.

'Mom!' I yell. 'I'm going for a party today!'

She appears, looking sort of busy. As usual, Elle is clinging to her. 'Of course, dear, have fun.'

Elle seems surprised at my plan to go out. It surprises her so much that she leaves my mother and hazily moves towards me. 'Are you going with that boy?' she asks, knowing Romeo from the times he has come around here.

'Yeah, he's my ride,' I say, realizing that I'm having a normal conversation with her. She coughs, her beautiful face lines for a second. On closer inspection, I notice that her beautiful skin isn't that beautiful any more. It seems to be clouded with spots.

'I could help you,' she says shyly. Our roles should be reversed. I should be saying that and she should be gracefully accepting, excited that her sister is going to help her for her first party. But things never happen as they're supposed to.

I consider refusing but the desperation in her eyes makes me agree. 'Sure.'

She squeals and flounces off to my – our – mom.

'That kid,' I say and shake my head at her retreating figure.

At around eight, Elle appears in my room again and I close the book I'm reading. 'Hi,' she says nicely. 'I'm here to dress you up. Let me do your face. Just close your eyes.'

I close my eyes but I can't help wonder what would happen if I was in Elle's place and if we were real sisters. She keeps lathering my face with something and after a while she lets me open my eyes. I look at my face in the mirror and I look … good. I mean, not to be conceited, but *really good*. 'Thanks,' I say, meaning it.

She smiles and makes an attempt at a joke, 'Go get your Romeo.' Then she runs off somewhere, probably to my mother.

I get up and roam around for a while before the clock strikes nine. I suddenly feel an incredible sense of déjà vu. Dread takes over. The Rudimental concert, I think and feel faint. We all know how that ended. I try to calm myself but I can't help it, I'm hyperventilating. I run to the kitchen and grab a glass of water and drink it down quickly. A car honks outside and I rush out. I'm sweating but my face still looks a million bucks.

'Wow,' says Romeo when he sees me. For some weird reason, his face calms me down and I relax.

'Elle did it,' I say, giving her credit. 'So who's your date?'

'You are.' He smiles deviously.

I give him a look and say, 'Seriously, who are you a-courting?'

He shyly whispers, 'Rose.'

I laugh. 'You can have anyone and you choose her. She doesn't even like you that much.'

He frowns. 'I can't help it. I'm infatuated. Ralph said she's into me.'

'I'll ask her.'

He puts his hands on the steering wheel and gives me a death glare. 'You'll do no such thing.'

We drive in silence until we reach the party. It's at his classmate's house and the outside is covered in toilet paper. Everyone is dressed in casual clothes and dancing to a popular tune. We go in and everyone stops dancing and the music magically stops. 'It's her!' someone whispers in the crowd.

'Hi, I felt like eating tonight, so here I am,' I scream to the crowd. They stare at me, not blinking. 'Who wants to party?' I yell and everyone shouts 'yes' in approval and the music turns back on and everyone is dancing again.

'You owned that crowd!' Romeo compliments me.

'Well, actually, owning them wouldn't be legal because we live in a society…' I realize he's not listening. Then I see who's approaching us: Rose. She's surrounded by her lackeys but she comes towards us. Her surprise at seeing me is hidden quite well. There's a look of complete devotion on Romeo's face when she greets us. I grin evilly, feeling mean. 'So, Rose, I heard you have your eyes on someone.'

She blushes while her lackeys exchange glances. Romeo tries his hardest to remain cool while giving me his strongest death glare. 'Yeah, it's Romeo's friend, Mark.' I nod, not really caring because all these names are becoming too much for me. Remembering Chor (a nickname) is a task. Romeo has a look of utter desperation on his face.

'But Mark's with Elizabeth,' he says in a last attempt to make Rose fall in love with him.

'I know,' she says and winks.

I smile back at her and laugh. 'Theft is not approved of.'

She laughs too but doesn't notice Romeo's wounded look.

'I'm going to get a drink. Juliet, join me,' Romeo commands and I wave bye to Rose. He drags me to the drinks table and punches my arm. 'Why did you do that?' he asks.

'Relax, at least you know the truth now,' I say to him and rub my arm.

'Couldn't you let me dream? You are evil, Juliet,' he says and turns away.

'I didn't know she was Romeo's wife-to-be,' I say sarcastically.

'You didn't have to do that, you know. You could have asked her privately and never told me.'

'That would be lying,' I say, but I don't look at him.

'You've never had a problem with that before!' he says and scoops up some punch.

'That's spiked with alcohol.'

'I don't care,' he says and takes a long sip.

I put his cup down. 'But I do.'

'No, you don't! That's the thing, Juliet, you don't care about anyone.'

'I'm sorry,' I say and it must have sounded genuine because he pipes down.

'Come, meet my friend,' he says and leads me to Chor.

'Hi,' I say, already bored. He's good-looking but nothing exciting.

'Hey,' he says, but he's also a little scared.

'Let's dance!' I say and grab a cup of the punch, forgetting or rather remembering there's alcohol in it. I feel a bit woozy as I point to Romeo and say, 'You're the designated driver, so no drinking for you.' Then I walk on to the dance floor, not sure how to dance.

I chat with Chor but my heart isn't in it. We acknowledge that there is no chemistry but keep dancing. At around eleven Romeo comes up to me and I nod at him. 'Ro-me-o,' I sing, feeling the effects of the alcohol.

'Juliet, are you okay?' he asks and then he notices the cluster of glasses on the floor. There are fifteen, but five are not mine. 'Let's get you home,' he says and leads me to his car.

I lie down in the back but I feel like dancing. Unfortunately, Romeo doesn't stop so I'm stuck with shaking in the back. Once we reach home, I quietly open the front door but I see my mom and Elle are still up. I'm so infused with alcohol that I think I see Mom inject something into Elle and she smiles, dazed. I shake my head and I see no injection. I probably imagined it.

'Mommy!' I say and run to my room instead of her open arms. I hear Romeo talking from my room.

'She drank a lot; I'm sorry I didn't keep track of her.'

'Thank you, Romeo, she'll be fine, don't worry. You didn't drink though?'

'No, I had to drive.'

I fall into bed and embrace the pillow. 'Soft,' I purr before falling asleep.

I wake up the next morning with an aching head, a head blasting from my alcohol overdose. 'I'm never drinking again,' I moan when Mom comes in with a gigantic glass of blue liquid.

She gives me a small pill and says, 'Have the aspirin and the drink, dear. They'll make you better.'

'Thanks,' I say and have what my mom is offering. She smiles when she sees me accept her kindness.

My headache weakens and I feel a lot better, but after some time a different sort of headache comes on. It's like that terrible time I got sick when I had just returned to the house after being banished. I feel sweaty and sick but at least the headache is a gentle throb which won't go away, instead of feeling like a wall has collapsed on my head.

Romeo calls a little later to check on me. 'Hey, Juliet, you okay now?'

'Why didn't you stop me?' I complain.

'You didn't ask me to, and besides, you completely disappeared.'

'I was in the middle of the dance floor!'

He laughs and that makes my headache reduce a bit. 'Fine,' he says, '*I* disappeared.'

'Where did you go?' I ask, curiosity getting the better of me.

'I was joking,' he says, but I can tell he's lying.

'Please tell me!' I plead. I have to plead a few more times for him to finally break. 'I got a gift.'

I try to hide my disappointment. 'For whom?'

'You,' he says mildly. 'Remember your dad's suitcase? Well, I found it when I went to the woods. It's a bit muddy but … I don't really think you care.'

'You went to the woods without me?' I ask, gently massaging my temples.

'Only you would ask that after I did you a gigantic favour.'

'My Romeo!' I say in mock distress and we both laugh. It feels good to just relax, even with this headache. I hear someone calling for him and he says bye.

I've been feeling better emotionally, but physically I'm not doing that well. I need to take breaks from walking up the stairs and my face has been getting paler and spots are beginning to appear on it. Still, it's hard to distinguish between earlier me and new me. Elle, however, has been changing completely. I haven't just noticed; I've been seeing the changes progress and increase over a period of time. Her usual bright ringlets have become straight and her hair is falling so much, it clogs up the drain. Her face is very spotted and her eyes a sleepless red. She isn't the perfect angel she once looked like.

I am not tired at night so it takes me a while to fall asleep. My mom had given me another blue liquid to help me sleep but it has just increased my headache. I've been trying so hard to be nice but the headaches bring out my irritability. Nevertheless, if the headaches are too much then I become the most helpless person on earth. I stuff the pillow over my ears. I change position again and again, hoping that each will be the last time I move. I keep trying to blink, even with my eyes closed. Suddenly I hear my door open and I get up, happy to have a reason for 'waking up'. I expect it to be my mom with more remedies, but it's the shaking silhouette of a twelve-year-old Elle. She's shivering and I can hear sobs. I throw the covers back and lead the trembling girl to my bed. I seat her down and question her.

'What's wrong?'

She is silent.

'Is it something you ate?'

No answer.

'Something you drank?'

I guess.

She nods but only a little, and I feel her forehead. 'You're burning up,' I say with apprehension. She says something incoherently, trying to tell me what's wrong. 'Should I take you to Mom?'

She violently shakes her head and I'm shocked at this reaction. Elle follows my mother everywhere, she seems to be surgically attached to her. I'm surprised she even came to me. Why won't she go to Mom? Did she drink something she wasn't supposed to? I don't bother to question her; no doubt stony silence will be the answer. I feel her forehead again and I'm not kidding when I say you could boil water on it. She looks pale and clammy and her expression is that of a wounded animal. 'You need a doctor,' I advise her and she shakes her head by a fraction of an inch. 'Hey,' I say, and bring her close. 'You're going to be okay.'

We sit in sisterly embrace for a while until Elle gets up. She runs out of the doorway, but just before she disappears I hear her say something in her drained and drowsy voice: 'Juliet, you're next.'

I gape at her retreating figure, not sure whether to go after her. I decide against it. I'm next for what? Eternal damnation? Don't worry, Elle, people call me the Devil, I look after eternal damnation. I slap myself, how can I be joking when my adopted sister just looked like death and told me I was up next for whatever happened to her? I decide to ignore what she said. She seems ill, people say silly things when they are ill. Still, I can't seem to shake off the uneasiness. I go to bed but not to sleep because that's even harder to do than before.

In the morning I go for breakfast, unusually calm. My mom smiles when she sees me and provides me with eggs and bread. I take a bite, making sure to enjoy every bite. But the bread tastes thin and worn and the eggs look like someone vomited them out. I try to stuff it down, not wanting to disappoint Mom.

'Where's Elle?' I ask, noticing her absence.

My mom looks a bit surprised but not shocked at my question. 'She's in the hospital.'

I am completely taken by surprise here. 'How are you so calm?'

'We're going to visit her right after breakfast.'

I nearly choke on my eggs. 'Did she go during the night?' For some reason, I don't mention Elle's visit to me.

'Yes,' she says mildly. 'Her temperature went up to 106 degrees. So I took my baby to the hospital.'

'I'm done, let's go.'

She looks down at my plate, still full of eggs and a slice of measly bread. Basically, I haven't eaten any of it because it tastes disgusting but Mom assumes something else. 'Juliet, don't worry, your sister is going to be okay. You can eat, she won't mind. She's not actually hurt.'

I nod and stuff some of the yolk into my mouth. 'Let's go now.'

'I knew that somewhere in your black, devil heart, you care for her.'

I actually feel the vomit in my mouth now. Why is she still calling me a devil? Haven't I been good? I've been trying.

Mom has bags packed with Elle's favourite books and her doll. I don't remind her that Elle is twelve, not five.

I feel queasy when the hospital comes into view. I hate this place, everything bad that happens happens here. I keep a one-track mind as we walk down the pale off-white hallways, each corridor resembling the other. We walk in and I feel panic rise as we pass the ICU. I subtly close my eyes and walk with my other senses. No one notices that I'm walking blind.

Really, the ICU means a grim chance of surviving. And we're going deeper and deeper into it. We finally reach Elle's wing, and her face looks frayed and she closes her eyes tightly when she sees us.

My mother whispers excitedly to me, 'Juliet, I can't wait to take care of Elle. Oh, my poor baby!'

I look at her in complete horror. First, she's excited in a hospital, and second, she thinks she's going to take care of

Elle? She bustles off to talk to the doctors and nurses, who are looking at Elle with great admiration. Admiration? I go over to Elle, who opens one eye and relaxes when she sees me.

'Hey,' I say softly and she smiles a little.

'Hey. Listen, be careful, you're next,' she says as if on repeat.

'Next for what?' I ask impatiently and she flinches.

Her blood pressure goes up and that's dangerous for her. I step away before anyone can come shouting at me for harming her. My mother comes back with a doctor by her side; she looks forlorn, having none of the joy she had a few minutes ago.

'They say I can't take care of Elle and I'm supposed to go home and wait. I can take care of my own daughter,' she mutters.

Adopted, but I don't correct her.

The doctor turns to me and says, 'Can I speak to you alone for a while?'

My mom isn't paying attention; she's bending down to look at Elle. I follow the doctor to a room from where Elle and my mom are still visible. The doctor seems younger than the usual doctors. At least his hair hasn't fallen out. He looks concerned and sits down while I continue to stare out at Elle.

'Your sister is very strong,' he comments.

This time I make the correction, 'Step sister.'

He looks irritated when I say that. 'She's been digesting and swallowing poison for a while now.'

'Poison? How is that possible?'

'I have an idea but that's irrelevant right now. See, this poison is a bit different. It's been infused with caffeine and that's very clever. Caffeine can decrease the effect of poison and it creates a fake high before the poison takes effect. When the poison takes effect, the caffeine's depression phase does too. If someone didn't continuously nurse the person suffering this, then it could lead to death.'

'I see,' I say, genuinely interested.

'In this case, I'd say your mother nursed the girl.'

'That's right. Sometimes what you just described happens to me too.'

His face lights up. 'Look, Juliet, isn't it? Well, Juliet, can you tell me, is your mother a needy person?'

I grunt, not wanting to admit anything. 'How is my mother relevant?'

'Your mother is everything here. Does she enjoy taking care of you?'

'She's my mother.'

'You're avoiding the question.'

A smartass. 'Obsessively so,' I say truthfully.

He looks down at his notes and says softly, 'These poisons were taken in at intervals, allowing the person to recover before being poisoned again. These kinds of reports are only seen in psychological cases. Of course, it could be a coincidence, but I believe your mother has something to do with it.'

'Tell me more.'

'See, what happens is a psychological wonder. Some people find pleasure in caring for someone close to them. So this person, normally a mother or father, more a mother, wants their child to need them. They are just searching for a reason to exist; taking care of someone is a purpose. They usually take care of children. Excessively take care. Elle was probably healthy and didn't need your mother, so your mother decided to change that. She probably enjoys Elle needing her, and therefore does this. I found it strange that she so badly wanted to take care of her daughter. She thought we'd let her be one of the nurses; that's when I began to wonder.'

I take everything in but I still have a question. 'Why Elle and not me? I'm her real daughter.'

He tugs at his chin. 'I imagine you're harder to take care of. You probably rejected her help, making her she move on to Elle.'

I nod but I feel a bit jealous. Does a pretty person get everything, even love? Okay, so maybe I rejected Mom and left her after Dad died and never asked for her help but ... Okay, how could I possibly want my own mother to poison me?

He glances at me. 'Putting these people in jail is harder...'

'*Jail?*' I interject.

'I'm sorry, but we have to. Harming another person is crime. I'm truly sorry, but we have to do this. For your own safety, unless you have any more siblings, you'll be next.'

So this is what Elle meant. She was trying to warn me. My heart warms up to her and I feel light-headed. 'Fine,' I say gruffly.

'Your mother will come up with a reason and a good lawyer to get out of this mess, so it has to been done discreetly. She needs to be surprised. If we put pressure on her then without knowing it, she'll admit to everything.'

'So how do we surprise her into confessing?' I ask warily.

'We need you to die.'

I choke, about to punch the doctor before he starts talking again. 'I have a pill which momentarily creates the illusion of a heart not beating. You just have to lie down. You can close your eyes and act dead.'

'I can do that but how will that make her confess?'

'She'll confess because – remember, I told you? – these people are nervous. Ready to blow up at anything and everything, so this will scare her into confessing. I'm sure it will work,' he says confidently.

He turns away but I call him back. 'Listen, is it ... is it normal to write words on your own skin?'

He smiles a knowing smile. 'As long as you don't hurt yourself.'

I call out that I'm asking for a friend but he's already gone.

On the ride back home, my mother seems fairly happy. I know I agreed to help the doctor, but I can't help but wonder if he's wrong.

'Mom, do you like taking care of me?' I ask straightforwardly.

'More than anything,' she says and pauses to look at me. I almost throw up from the amount of love in her eyes. 'You and Elle are my life. Your dad used to be my life but...'

The mention of my dad brings to my mind the continuous fevers he used to get. The chest pains he used to complain of and yet he went all around the world. *Anything to get away from home.*

Mom turns into the driveway and we get out. I don't say anything to Mom and run up to my room the second she opens the door. Running that fast dizzies me and I rest in bed, lying down and facing up. I feel a longing and I look to my answer. My black marker. I pick it up, slowly relishing its touch. I missed it. 'What is self-control?' I murmur to myself, grinning slightly. I put it to my skin and write an endless number of words. They describe my conflicted feelings right now. I finally feel satisfied and put the marker down. I'm not sure how to get my mom to confess what she did. I don't know how to pressure her into saying what will ruin her. But I've learnt that your enemies don't ruin you, you ruin yourself. I pace my room, keeping my footing light and easy so I'm not heard. There's a little sunlight coming in from the windows. It's hard to avoid the sun, although every moment feels like it is night. 'Romeo,' I whisper. I feel like listening to his voice. I pick up the phone and he picks up on the second ring.

'Hey,' he says, having an instant soothing effect on me. 'So I'm guessing you're bored.'

'Your deduction is good.'

'So since you're not doing anything either, the woods?'

I think for a second. I'm going to have the confrontation at night, so why not enjoy now? 'Five minutes.' Soon I'm speeding away to the woods without notifying my mother. She'll probably worry, but I don't care. I run to the canopied forest where Romeo waits.

It's dark there. It represents my mind. 'So why are we here today?'

His casual mood instantly disappears and is replaced with concern. I hate and love how he can detect my mood. 'What's wrong?' he asks.

'Nothing,' I say but my voice betrays me.

He sighs. 'You know you can't hide anything from me.'

He's right. 'I just wish I wasn't such a coward,' I say wearily.

'You're not a coward. You're the strongest person I know,' he says. 'There's a difference between strong and devoid of emotion. You can be a bit heartless but you can express emotion. And you're not a coward. What happened to the friend who died in the fire?'

I'm not sure if I can trust him. I was a coward back then too. I don't know if I'll ever be able to tell anyone what really happened. What I did was just ... *too much.*

'You'll hate me,' I whisper.

He doesn't say anything. He takes my hand and holds it.

'It was a normal day,' I begin, trying not to let my voice break. 'Her name was Maya. I didn't know her that well at first, but when I got to know her ... she was a crazy person, you know. She always took the hard route because it was fun. It didn't matter if she had to work, she wasn't lazy at all. She was an ideal person. She could go to any college she wanted. She was at the culmination of her life, everything was going great. She was just so full of life.'

I pause to see if he's listening and he is, carefully, precisely. 'Then that day, 21 March, the terrible fire. She was supposed

to be meeting with school representatives that day. I was in
detention for talking back to a teacher but I was hungry. So she
took me along, irrelevant of whether or not she'd get caught.
We went for lunch and no one noticed me, no one saw me.
It was like I wasn't there. We sat down, everyone fascinated
by their own mediocre lives. The chatter was so loud that no
one noticed a match fall to the floor. On the floor there were
curtains, the curtains touched the electric circuits and you can
guess what happened next. The fire was so vibrant, so loud,
exactly like Maya. She was captivated by the fire, awestruck
even. Everyone else was hurrying out, there was a stampede all
around. Everyone wanted to live, they wanted to be the ones who
lucked out. The sound was so loud, everyone was just running.
I was so scared, I didn't know whether or not I was going to
die. She wasn't scared, though, she was glaring at everyone. She
told me we needed sand, but I wasn't thinking very much …
I wanted to live, no matter what. So I pulled her against her
will towards the emergency exit. The exit was crowded because
the fire was rapidly beginning to grow, its flames huge. Once
I got closer to the window I could see medics outside. They
were in a frenzy with so many burnt kids. The fire trucks could
be heard coming but there was no hope for those still inside.
But I had to live. I just had to live. So I fought through the
crowd and Maya followed me. For once, she followed me and
I got us out. I cut myself against the glass in the process but I
got us out. The smoke from the fire had gotten to us, though,
and we needed oxygen. And I … I noticed that there was only
one oxygen tank left. She collapsed to the ground, worn out,

tired, exhausted but I had energy. I needed to live so I called the medic over. "She's dead, Maya's dead," I told the medic and he looked at me, distraught. Then I fell and he took me to one of the camps where I was given immediate attention.'

I can't bring myself to look at Romeo; tears are streaming down my face. 'So I basically killed my friend. I could have saved her. I didn't have to say that she was dead but I needed to be sure that they'd help me first. I'm … I'm ashamed of what I did to survive but … I killed her. And to this date people think I was in the detention room, nowhere near the lunch hall. Her parents could cry for her, but I'm not allowed to feel sad when I'm the reason she died. Please don't tell anyone, I'm a coward I know, but I'm sorry. I really am the devil.'

Romeo holds me firmly. His eyes don't carry hate or disgust, but sympathy. 'You're not a devil. It wasn't your fault; you did what you had to. She was probably long gone anyway. You're lucky you made it. If she collapsed before you then it was because of heart failure and suffocation. You couldn't have helped her anyway. And you *are* allowed to feel sad.' He wipes away my tears, devotion in his eyes. 'Crying isn't showing weakness. It has been a sign from when you were born that you're alive.'

He's accepted so much of me and he's made me better. I wonder if I can show him what's on my skin. I decide I can, he should expect it from me. I think he can heal me. I take off my jacket and pull up my jeans. The words ring vibrant and clear.

Unwanted. Removable. Waste. Dead. Wrong. Dying. Unrequited. Lies. Gone. Had been. Pain. Time.

The look on his face is not of disgust. Nor of excessive care like my mother's. This is different; it's like he *actually* understands my pain without going through it. 'I am a devil,' I tell him again.

'You're beautiful,' he says, his eyes trailing over me and reading all the words. 'You're not the devil, you're a fallen angel.'

A fallen angel – that makes sense. I'm not a devil but I'm the one god sent away. I'm a disgrace but I'm still good and holy. That's when the true meaning of good and bad comes to me. I stand up and look at Romeo fondly, 'Thank you, you saved me.' And I mean it.

He knows it. 'I think you're going to be fine now,' he says and we watch the sun set.

So much time has passed. That's when a little doubt slithers into my mind about what I must do next: to get my mother to confess. The pill is in my drawer next to my marker. We sit together and stare up at the canopy. The leaves sparkle and dance but it's all fake. A routine. It's all very picturesque, but finally, we both know we have to go. I consider telling him about my mother but decide not to. Enough grief for one day, don't you think?

I walk back home, dread returning to my body but not settling completely. When I get to my wooden door, I'm literally shaking. But I need to do this to survive. I can't let her poison me just so she can kiss me better after. Once I'm in, I see she's sitting by the couch. A tall blue drink is near her. I almost double up but remain calm. I run to my bedroom and fetch the pill, in case I'll need it. Then I turn on the recorder, trying not to feel intimidated by it.

'You could have told me you were going out,' Mom says, once I'm back down. She hasn't offered the glass yet.

'Sorry, it won't happen again.'

We sit in silence, and I play with my fingers, not sure where this conversation is going. 'How're you feeling?' she asks finally.

'Fine as rain,' I say and she grimaces as expected.

'Here,' she says, giving me the blue glass. 'Drink up.'

I decide to make my first move now. 'Is this the reason Elle's in the hospital?'

'What do you mean?' she asks shortly. 'Elle's being sick has got nothing to do with me.'

'Actually, you've been poisoning us,' I tell her slowly. This is a huge gamble but I see the reaction immediately.

'How dare you say that? You dirty girl. I let you back into my house and this is how you repay me?'

'It's not my fault you find pleasure in poisoning us and then helping us get better.'

'You sick creature, you devil!'

'Actually, I'm not a devil, that's you. I'm a *fallen angel*. There's a difference.'

'I never did anything to you or Elle!' she screams at me.

'You did something to me, Elle and Dad.'

She falls to the couch and I take this as a sign to keep talking. 'Dad used to complain of pains and your eyes used to light up every time he was sick. When I was sick, you'd squeal with joy. When we were healthy, you disappeared from view. How long had you been poisoning him?' I ask, the disgust clear in my voice.

'I didn't hurt him, I loved him.'

'Yes, you loved him, you loved him too much. So much that the car crash was probably the best thing that happened to him.'

Mom starts to cry, she's sobbing relentlessly but she isn't confessing.

'You killed him,' I say, trying to force her into saying something. 'You're now killing Elle and me too.'

She sobs and says something that I can't make out.

'You know what,' I say and run up to my room and fetch my dad's suitcase.

Yes, I still haven't opened it. Although I more or less know what the souvenir is. Not a souvenir, probably a note. I return downstairs and my mom is clutching her head in a state of panic and indecision. I open it and show her a note; so I was right. It has one sentence that I quickly scan.

'Do you want to know what Dad said?' I ask her and she whimpers. 'He said, "The one who loves you the most will kill you." I don't think I have to explain what that means, you know what it means.'

She whimpers again, 'I didn't do anything!'

I decide to use my last weapon. 'So if I have this drink,' I say, and pick up the blue liquid, 'nothing will happen to me?'

'Nothing,' she promises but I can see the fear in her eyes.

'Fine,' I say and cleverly make sure the pill goes into my mouth when she puts her head down to howl. The doctor had told me that it'll take the pill a few seconds to work. Then I do my best imitation of someone dying and fall to the ground. I keep my eyes closed so it's like I'm sleeping but the illusion of death is complete.

'No!' she yells and clutches me. 'That wasn't supposed to happen.'

Terrified, she checks my heartbeat, which cannot be felt; the pill lowers the heartbeat so you can't feel it with your hand.

'You're not supposed to die! I never meant to hurt any of you. I just wanted to take care of you. I just wanted to make sure you were okay! You can't die, Juliet. You may be the difficult one, but I still need you. Elle's too weak and she can't be poisoned for a while. How am I supposed to go through life without taking care of you?'

I smile and cry at the same time in my head. My head is becoming cloudy again, the calm in it is slowly disappearing. The doctor was right. When you put enough pressure on her, she'll crack and spill. She's like a rubber band you pull too hard. I don't move in case she might say something more. Then I hear the voice that is my lifeline.

The one I will never be able to live without. Romeo. 'Hey, Aunty, is Juliet here?' he asks.

I open my eyes slightly and see Romeo's face flash with concern when he sees my mother crying and me collapsed on the ground. 'Juliet's dead, I killed her,' she says and I get all the confession the doctor would require.

Still, I'm paralysed and can't move or get up. Romeo rushes to me, tears in his eyes, and he checks my heartbeat. I'll be dead to him too. I so badly want to get up and confirm I'm alive, but I'm not able to. He then whispers to me, while my mother howls in the corner, 'Juliet, I can't live without you. Please don't die! I can't live without you. I was trying to be perfect and you made me alive. I was searching for perfection but you taught me perfection can come in many forms. For me, perfection came in the form of a fallen angel. You made me laugh and cry, but most importantly you taught me how to live. How am I supposed to live without you? I have to join you! I can't go on with all these unimportant things. Finally, I'll become a lawyer and I'll achieve everything I ever wanted, but that's not what I want. I need to be with you, I owe that to you.'

I hear him rush to the kitchen and I try my hardest to get up and stop him but I can't move. I didn't know the pill paralyses you for so long. I hear him come back and I know he's holding a knife or some other sharp object. I didn't know he loved me, I didn't know any of these things. I didn't know I mattered enough to die for. In that moment, I know I have memories and all of those are of Romeo and of my dad. I can't be responsible for another death. I open my eyes as wide as I can but he's not looking at me. His eyes have a glazed look and he holds the knife to his chest. He's in a state of irrationality and I can't stop him.

'It's no coincidence that our names had created the greatest love story ever. It's no coincidence that Romeo met Juliet. It's fate.'

Then he stabs himself and falls over me. I want to get up and force my mother to take him to the hospital but I can't. My mother is useless and she's crying in a corner. My whole house is filled with death, sorrow, grief and after a few moments I can move.

No! I yell mentally. This is a second too late, he's already gone. Romeo, my lifeline, is dead. He still looks as perfect as ever but he's no longer full of life. All of my sorrow is out in the open and the pouch in my mind explodes. I allow myself to cry. This is one death that I can cry for.

When I look at Romeo I feel an emotion I didn't know I was capable of feeling. Love. What is life? I wonder again in this moment. And I hear Romeo's answer, the only one that matters. '*He drew a circle that shut me out – heretic, rebel, a thing to flout. But love and I had the wit to win: we drew a circle that took him in!*'

I let grief flood me. I look at Romeo again. I know I can't live without him and I know it's wrong to depend on someone that much. I used to scorn Shakespeare's story of Romeo and Juliet. It was stupid. Why would they die for each other? But now I realize that love does that to people. They can't imagine life without one another. So if they can't be together in life, then death will have to do.

When I was without Romeo I was dying, he loved me back to life. I had no idea Romeo felt the same way about me. No, I shake my head. It's wrong to depend on him so much, but I can't survive without Romeo. And like our earlier versions, if we can't be together in life, then death will have to do. It's something new and unexplored, something infinite.

I pick up the knife, my hands shaking for what I'm about to do. I hold it to my chest and Mom's yell is an incoherent background noise. Then I push it in and I see Romeo waiting for me. *True love conquers death.* The last thought in my head before I lose myself to the one I love is: It is no coincidence that Romeo met Juliet. It's fate.

In death, I can finally see. Romeo and I will forever be entwined; death cannot do us apart. Even after everything and everyone dies, love remains.

A VACANCY

The word was 'miserable' and it was a word that ceased to be used in my family after my sister died. This was never made explicit, but somehow, my father and I understood that this was not a word we could say if we wanted to protect the sanity of our household.

It hadn't been like this when my sister was still alive, when she and my mother would sleep in the same bed, and I would listen through the wall. Their laughter, the twinkling of fairy lights, their whispers smooth like velvet. Every night, I dreamed of being in between them; my sister crumbling away so my hands could finally weave themselves into my mother's hair, and I could rest in the comfort of her gentle breaths like my sister did; intertwined with my mother, my chest rising with hers and deflating at the same time. But every time I tried, my mother would not look at me, and would instead search for my sister, her body swaying away from me, her arms flailing out in front of her, trying to reach my sister as my hand tried to grab on to her.

My mother loved to sing; and she did this only for herself, but sometimes I would sit with my back against her closed door and listen to her heavy voice, the voice with which she spoke to my sister. She would sing sad songs: songs about a girl's lover leaving her, songs about dying, songs about never being good enough. These were songs we'd often heard, blasting out of a small pink stereo, narrow hips swaying, dolls clutched tightly.

I wanted to open the door and see what she looked like when she sang all by herself, but the door remained closed and my hands lay pressed against the wood, pushing the door as hard as I could but never so hard that it opened.

After my mother had finished singing, oblivious to my quiet breaths outside her door, she would come out of her room and pour a bottle of vodka into a ceramic mug as if its gentle edges and innocent appeal would change the reality of the poison inside. My mother would pour the vodka into my mouth every evening after my sister died, like it was our medicine. I would open my lips eagerly and take in every drop she poured down my throat because even though it tasted bitter, like cleaning acid, I understood what my mother was trying to do. She was hoping that, as the burning liquid spread through our bodies, it would clean away our insides and wipe away our memories.

Sometimes I wished my father would walk in on this ritual that my mother had begun, and see what was happening in his absence, but at the same time I hoped he would never come back at all. I found a sort of melancholy peace in my mother's accepting eyes when she thought she was cleansing me, changing me.

Once the monsoon started and it rained almost every evening, my father came home with a larger scowl on his face than usual. My father lived in a cloud of contempt and condescension ever since my sister had died, his nostrils flaring every time my mother and I tried to draw his attention towards us, his sighs passive-aggressive; the only way he could even look at us any more. My mother blamed his malicious compliancy on his being a businessman with a lot of work. 'Just his job, Tia,' she'd say and lightly jab my head as if trying to force me to understand that there was nothing wrong, and that the dark circles under his eyes, his late office hours and his second phone were only signs of the stress that came with his job. I wanted to tell my mother that she was blind, and that his tired, miserable face resembled hers, but I knew not to.

The one thing my mother requested of me, once my sister died, was silence; both in my voice and in my mind.

In school, I smiled the way my mother wanted her daughter to smile: lips first curving upwards then outwards, eyes crinkled just the right amount, with the hope and optimism of a child. I practised it whenever I could, and flashed it at my mother often, even though she could not bear to look at me. I practised more after that, stretching my mouth with my fingers and pulling hard, because I knew the only way my mother would be able to love me would be when I finally learnt to smile the way she wanted.

One Friday afternoon when school ended early and I walked to the main door of my house, I could see my mother sitting on the ground of our yard, staring right at me through the glass. Her gaze was that of misery, but her mouth was upturned in a sort of grin, as if she was trying to show me that I had to smile as well. Her arms looked rail-thin and lay by her side, limp and flaccid, as if she was trying to remember how to use them. She looked away from me and stared at the grass she was sitting on, and then swiftly, in one motion, started tearing out the weeds. Her fingers dug deep into the soil and she screamed without any sound, her mouth open and her eyes wide in shock as she realized that she could dig for all time but would not find what she was looking for.

I turned away then and ran because there was nothing else I could do. The air turned bitter as I slowed down and I waved my hands around me, trying to ward off my sister, because she was still here and she was still with me. My mother, my sister and I would be caught in this triangle forever, I realized, unless I could swallow my mother and keep her inside me, coursing through my blood, pumping my heart. This would be the only way I could keep her protected from my sister.

I remembered how, when I was five years old and my sister was not yet born, I would try to gulp down my mother's arm, my toothless gums grabbing at her skin, biting down. *Sweet, sweet baby, sweet baby, sweet baby*, my mother would croon when I'd try to guzzle her up, her cinnamon scent, one I tried to find in a perfume years later.

A Vacancy

The first thing I saw when the warmth of the crowded street hit me was my father's face, gazing at something in the distance, sad and lonely. The second thing I saw was the back of a tall woman who looked to be my father's age, with long brown hair and a black dress. I understood everything then, even though I tried not to.

I tried to move closer to my father, my steps unsure, as I pushed through the backs and feet around me. The woman turned for a second and I saw her as she truly was — eyelashes long and dark, with cheeks like knives and a mouth pursed in effortless cool. She glanced at me for a second but her eyes soon lazily rolled over somewhere else, as if I was not worth more than a moment's gaze. I knew then that she was not my father's age, and that she was closer to my age than his. Youth shone out of her face, which, even though it had been painted over, was just as raw and naive as mine.

'Dad.' My voice came out harsh, harsher than my mother would have liked.

The woman didn't turn, but my father looked at me warily, his eyes following mine, as if he had almost been expecting this, knowing it was going to happen.

'Dad?' I said again, my voice a croak this time, scratchy after the strength of my first utterance, my energy sapped. It was tiring to speak after my mother had explained to me that my voice was no longer my own, and my mind was being replaced, and my body had to be changed if I wanted to be her daughter.

My father sighed and rested his eyes on mine as he whispered to the woman, then shook his head at her as she raised an eyebrow. I tried to forget the lost look he'd had on his face that had disappeared when he saw the woman with the dark eyes and baby face.

He came towards me and gripped my shoulder and I could smell the woman's perfume on him, mixed with his own cologne. 'C'mon, Olivia, let's get you home.'

When we got back, my mother looked perfect, perched on our pristine sofa, watching the TV screen. She was wearing a white dress with golden pearls that hung around her neck so tightly, I wondered how she could breathe. Her long, thin fingers, which were adorned with bright red rubies and emeralds, kept pulling at her skin, as if trying to pierce through. I wanted to stop her, to touch her, but she remained focused on the TV, which she hadn't even turned on.

'Back so early, Dan? How was work? Did Chris come in today?' My mother's tone was serene and polite as she slathered cream on her body. I wanted to bite her neck just then, and feel her creamy flesh against my tongue, so soft and supple, melting like sugar in my mouth. Then I would be able to taste the love that my sister used to draw from her, only then would my mother slip into me. Only then would I be my mother's daughter.

My father's voice was jagged as he spoke. 'Eva, Chris quit, he's working with Elon Electrics now. I told you that a month ago.' My father pulled at my mother's shoulder. His eyes were red like they had been since my sister had died. 'Eva!'

My mother stood up nervously but her voice was relaxed as she spoke and pointed at me. 'Dan, Tia has been a bad girl today. Her teacher called and said she was saying untruths in school. Making up stories. You have to punish her.' My mother moved forward and clutched my father's arm, her movements seemingly genuine, comforting. But then her hands were pulling at her eyelashes, and they were falling on the sofa, like thin, black feathers.

My father's voice was tender when he spoke, so tender that I felt like collapsing at his feet and begging him to speak that kindly to me. 'Eva, I'm not going to punish her.'

I would pull out her eyelashes one by one and place them in a jar to look at after they had been frozen and dried. Then I would softly ease her throat and pull out all thirty-two of her teeth, to keep in a second jar after they were cleaned and whitened. I would save her blood for last, and once she had been sucked dry of any liquid, and left bare and pruned, I would hug her, hold her tight and swallow her.

'Tia's been a bad girl, Dan. Be a man. Punish her. She spoke untruths, she lied about us. She's just trying to get attention. She told them she's dead, Dan. How absurd! Tell her school that. Tell them, Dan. Dan?' My mother's voice did not falter even once, her words continuous and eerily sweet, like the songs she loved to sing.

'Eva.' My father's voice was wavering, dithering, failing. 'Her name isn't Tia, you know her name, say her name. Her name isn't Tia, it is Olivia. You know that. She's your daughter. You have to know that.'

'Tia's talking too much, Dan, far too much. I don't understand what has happened to her. Why can't she be like she used to be? Why is she so sullen now?'

And then I understood why nobody could understand my mother was miserable. She sounded so steady and calm that it was impossible to even fathom a reality different from hers.

'No, Eva. Tia is dead. Tia is gone.' My father was crying in the way a father cries when he loses a child. 'Tia is dead, Eva.'

I wanted to dress my mother up in my dead sister's clothes, and wrap her in them so tightly that she wouldn't be able to feel anything at all. I wanted her, just for a moment, to be like me, a dead girl walking.

'Don't say things like that, Dan. If Tia actually dies, then you'll be sorry. I know you feel upset that Olivia is dead but I preferred Tia anyway. Tia is so sweet, pretty, smart, the perfect daughter. Olivia was too sullen, too angry. She talked too much, didn't she, Dan? I say good riddance to bad rubbish. Thank god we still have Tia.'

'Tia is dead, Eva. I can't keep saying this to you. Olivia's still here.' My father's voice shook as he tried to keep it firm. 'Olivia's here. We lost one, but we still have the other.'

My father gripped my shoulder as if trying to remind himself of who I was, trying not to be swayed by mother. I wanted to touch him and cry with him one last time before I became my mother's daughter, but I knew it was too late. I would rip my own skin off and pull out all my teeth and hair and place it all on my sister's body. Then we would be one, only then would I be her.

'Mom, Daddy's lying. He doesn't know anything any more. He was with some woman today and he was touching her. You're right, Mom, Olivia's dead. But I'm still here.'

A Vacancy

I felt happy, or at least what I hoped was happiness, as I tried to enjoy the light fluttering in my stomach as if something was churning and then bubbling down to my intestines. 'Don't you see, Mom? I'm your daughter, I'm your Tia. I'm anything you want me to be, anything, Mom, please!' I would pull my mother closer and she would hug me, shower me in love, bathe me in her adoration. For the first time in my life, I would be my mother's daughter.

My father looked at me as if he'd been slapped.

My mother spoke quickly, her tone light and lively. 'Clean your room, Tia, and don't run out on the road, you might get hit. Dinner's going to be late tonight.'

'But she did get hit. She got hit a month ago, we saw the truck, we saw it hit her, what are you trying to do!' My father's voice was a shout but to my mother and me it was nothing more than a whisper. And then his voice cracked. 'Tia's gone, but Olivia's still here.' He turned to me and scrunched his eyes together, as if trying to see. 'Is she still here?'

'And tell Lauren not to come over any more, I heard her mother gets drunk and I don't want you around that kind of family. You're my baby, Tia, I have to keep you safe.'

'But we went down to the police station, you told them you understood what had happened, you said it was fine, you said you understood. We came back and you hugged Olivia and you told her Tia was dead. I don't understand. I refuse to understand. What are you doing to Olivia?' My father's incredulity and his blatant disbelief of my mother made me wish I'd never found him on that street.

'Goodnight, Tia, I love you.' My mother's voice sounded exactly as I'd always wanted to hear it.

I smiled perfectly as she bent down to hug me, her hair falling over me, her eyes entranced by my beauty. Warmth exploded out of her body and shot into me like fireworks, so different from the cold limp creature I had felt in my arms when I had been Olivia. I drew my mother's body into me tightly, feeling her rumbling, gasping heart as I tasted the loveliness of her skin between my teeth.

LA MER

When they finally arrive at the swimming competition, the daughter's hands are melting and the mother's eyes are burning. The pool is too large, at least 100 metres in length, and is a sea filled with legs and arms and branches of bodies. The shouting is too loud and the outpour of frenzied, nervous words is too familiar as parents scream, 'Where is the sunscreen?' and 'Find your goggles!' and 'I'll have the camera out, I promise.'

The daughter looks up to the mother, wonders what she is thinking. Her mother's mouth is open and gaping, too vacant to be approached. Kids in varied colours of suits run around, flitting between spaces, suddenly falling into the pool and then sprinting out, impervious, laughing, shouting. The daughter tastes the chlorinated water on her lips before she undresses. Her shirt falling over her back, parting slightly to reveal the crimson skin held taut by a rubbery blue suit.

'Should've practised in a bigger pool,' the mother says, as she pulls the daughter to the bleachers, rearing her forward and seating her down in between green towels and energy drinks.

It smells of urine and Clorox everywhere and there is a constant ringing in the daughter's ears from the wailing around and she almost giggles, but her mother's hand on her shoulder reminds her that there is nothing to laugh about.

'Do you want to practise now, before it starts? You have twenty minutes. You could still practise your breaststroke.' The mother is so anxious that her voice has become husky and slow. It is almost soothing.

'I don't know if I can do this.' The daughter thinks she is screaming, but the mother can barely even hear her. 'I really don't know.'

'Don't be stupid. You're only nervous.'

'Mom. Please.'

'You're missing out on an important opportunity. You love to swim. Don't be rash.'

'Mom. Please.'

'This is just like you. You give up before you even try. It's impossible to make you do anything.'

'Mom. Please.'

The mother sighs.

The daughter waits.

By the next day, the daughter has chewed and bitten her fingers to the point where the side of each is bleeding. In school, the daughter sucks her fingers violently, almost devouring the dried metallic blood on the sides, a beast baring her fangs, licking her arms and trying to stop her hand from aching. It is no longer just an irritation: it has been transformed into a threat, a slice of agony, a retelling of torment. She fantasizes that she'll need anaesthesia, and she'll have about the twenty minutes of pure, uninterrupted rest, when her brain will no longer click and her insides will no longer churn, and all she'll feel is the humdrum swaying of her own shallow breathing. She will become a quiet, downy body. She will not be ruffled; she will not be waylaid. She'll be like a piece of thin, cool marble, a slate of stone, steadfast and rooted, she will not drown.

When it is lunchtime, the daughter cannot find her friends so she talks to the boy sitting alone at the back of the lunch hall. He is cutting his sandwich into parts. Three pieces, five, ten and so on, but he doesn't put any bread in his mouth.

The daughter asks him what he's doing, but he doesn't look up. That is when she notices just how long his lashes are, how lewd and dark and luscious, like tiny, outstretched beetle legs.

'Have you seen my friends?' she asks, but he's already gulped down the little bits of fried egg on his plate and it seems as if he's going to leave any second. 'My friends? I can't find them?' She remembers them telling her that they'd wait for her at lunch. She realizes they were lying.

He doesn't say anything, he only shifts around in his seat, squirming like the worms she's seen in her yard.

'Look, I only want to know about my friends, where are they?'

'I don't know, retard,' says the boy and guffaws, his nostrils flaring into two deformed, dented circles. *He's so ugly*, decides the daughter, staring at the boils and red pimples all over his face and the shaggy, spindly strands of hair that lie tucked behind his oily ears. He seems like he likes to burn things, and watch fires, and just dream about arson all day, and it is all so terribly funny that the daughter feels that if she doesn't laugh, she'll die.

'Stay away from me, you pyromaniac. Go molest your sister or something.'

The daughter giggles then and a soft, curious, hollow sound escapes her mouth and she feels the familiar wave of fury within her leap up and then slowly fizzle out, like a match that was struck but whose fire didn't quite stay. When she watches the boy scowl, grimace and leave, she feels so vulgar and loutish that she wonders if she should run away and spend a few nights in the streets, armed with only her foul mouth and uncouth limbs. She imagines what will happen if she is murdered while on the run, if she is disembodied, if she is dissected. She tries to picture her attacker sucking out the breath from her lungs, swallowing her whole as he stabs her in an alley, tearing apart her arms, breaking her elbows, slowly, dearly, crushing her neck. In that moment, they could be lovers exchanging a brief whimper of submission; her attacker to his dark urges, and she to her desire of a long, palliative rest.

The daughter almost follows the boy, she almost tries to stop him, to apologize, but she cannot. It is not even worth it to try.

When the daughter is home, her mother descends upon her like a vulture, her claws piercing into the daughter's skin, holding her captive, caged.

'I got an e-mail from your physics teacher. He said you told him you weren't going to be taking the final?'

The daughter tugs at the worn skin near her nails, and exhales as it falls to the floor, leaving behind a stinging, blurred sensation. 'I'm not.'

'Why?'

'Because I won't be here.'

'You have two months. I'll make sure you are. Don't be like this.'

'I won't be here.'

The phone rings. The mother glances. *Husband*, blinks the caller ID.

'It's Dad, he wants to talk to you.' The mother thrusts the phone at her daughter, arms outstretched, pleading.

'Hey, Dad … Yeah … No, I'm fine. I didn't swim, I didn't want to … I don't know who came first, I wasn't there. Yeah, school's going okay. I'm not sure if we have a new teacher. Look, maybe you should just talk to Mom.'

And the daughter is out: slipping through the cracks in the door, dashing through the walls and gliding into the evening mist. The daughter almost turns back, almost runs home because, all of a sudden, everything seems too menacing, too mean. The pointed trees look like obscure alien creatures lying in wait for her, and the road ahead seems too pointless, going on for miles. Still, white swirls of fog push the daughter forward, carrying her thighs up into the air and down. The daughter tries to remember her mother, tries to think of the ocean, which her mother claims to love, but she can only see the road in front of her, and she dreams of jumping up and touching the bruised, purple sky. She feels as weightless as the smog that surrounds her, and more lifeless than the hordes of fallen chips packets on the ground.

She thinks of throwing herself in front of a truck, an oncoming lorry; she thinks of watching the driver's sleepy eyes when he realizes what he has done. She imagines him going home to his wife and hugging her and making love to her while crying, crying because he has killed a child, crying because he cannot stop dreaming of the child's mother cursing him for stealing her child. She almost laughs. It is a foolish idea. A lorry would create too large a scene and she cannot bear to think of her face in the newspaper for weeks, pale and splotchy and faint for everyone to see.

She enters the nearest convenience store with the brightest green neon lights she has ever seen and the largest variety of porn magazines she has never truly noticed before. She stares at the man behind the counter, who is picking at the red lumps on his skin. Stares at the woman staring into the deep freezer in the frozen food section, her hands quivering over different brands of peas. The daughter retreats further into the store, to the very end where they keep the pastas and the cookies and the dry fruit, and she thinks of how she has never had more than twelve almonds in her life. She thinks of all the things she has never done. She has never shoplifted, never kissed more than two boys, never kissed a girl, never kissed her father, never met her grandfather, never had a best friend. She thinks of buying the stale bread she sees next to the spaghetti to give to her mother as an explanation for why she was out so long. She touches the slippery plastic, reads the expiration date and imagines herself telling her mother that she thinks there's something terribly wrong with her. She has Googled it before. She has Googled 'how to talk to your parents', but the only results that came up were on how to come out to your parents and she thinks about how much easier it would be if she were gay and, once her mother accepted her, she wouldn't have to worry about anything any more. The daughter can see that it is getting very dark outside and the deep orange and violet hues of the sky are slowly turning into a molten smarmy blue.

She tries to think of a reason for all of this, a reason for why she is so tired, for why it feels as if she is carrying a ten-kilo load on her back every day. She can't tell why she gets agitated so easily. Sometimes the mother tells her she's just pretending, that if the daughter was truly sad then she would cry and let it out and then she wouldn't be so lazy and impetuous any more. The mother tells her daughter that everyone is sad and that there's nothing special about it and that she's only being silly. The mother tells her daughter that everyone's emotions get too much for them sometimes and that everyone has days when they cannot contain their feelings.

The daughter doesn't know how to tell her mother that feeling too much is not the problem, it never has been. The daughter doesn't know how to tell her mother that she doesn't know how to feel, the daughter cannot tell her mother that she does not feel at all.

SCENES FROM AN AUTHOR'S LIFE

Shinie Antony

1 January 2013, an email exchange:

Darling R,

I'm sending you a few words below. Pls make a sentence and send it back to me. Just like the exercises I used to set for you when you were very small :-)

Archetype

Neophyte

Avuncular

Penitence

Pernicious

Love, as always and forever,

Mama

Mumsy Daisy,
She was the archetype of a lady with too many dreams, and not
enough good years left.

Afterword

I was a neophyte to the idea of adulthood.
I had never been the type of person who was avuncular
to children.
Penitence was what he felt at the brink of death.
I could slowly feel her pernicious pull on my conscience.
Love,
R

———•———

Rudrakshi Bhattacharjee, all of sixteen, tiptoed out of this world and into another sometime in 2017, leaving behind stories, poems, a novella and many unfinished novels.

In the few years that she laughed and lived and walked her dog and fell in love with math and science, Rudrakshi got a lot of reading and writing done. Model daughter, only child, straight-A student, junior golf champion, ardent swimmer, self-conscious singer ... hers was a path of relentless questioning and observation. And both infuse her prose and poetry with an intellectual restlessness that is at once open and veiled.

Sitting with her stories strewn all around me, bits and pieces of her fiction – some long, some just a line, and her poetry, both finished and unfinished, I grew feverish with the discovery of so rare a voice. Her mother, an old friend, had gathered Rudrakshi's words from everywhere: journals that published them, her computer, her notebooks, her diary, scraps of paper she'd scribbled on ... Word flowing into word so alive with meaning and music, where craft and art overlap and fold into each other. What she wrote at the ages of thirteen and fourteen tears into the underbelly of intimacy – grief, jealousy, betrayal, infidelity, all arrogantly presumed adult terrain. Rudrakshi's complete mapping of her protagonists' emotional landscapes, filled out with empathy and not bystander curiosity, cures that particular arrogance.

As Andrew Gretes, who mentored Rudrakshi when she was selected for the 2017 Adroit Journal Mentorship Program, puts succinctly:

> There's a wonderful maturity in so many of Rudrakshi's sentences. When I read a line like, 'Sometimes she used to think her parents were like characters from different plays who came to rest under the same roof', the whole drama of being a child (half-offspring, half-spy) – our desperate quest to decode our parents – it all comes swirling back to me and gives me chills. Rudrakshi's fiction is littered with such lines.

As for me, I was struck time and again by how skinless language can be, heart-beating across the page. Words arranged in an inner arithmetic, almost ensouled. The title of the book, which comes from the first line of her story by the same name; it takes not just Mark and Antony but all those who people her fiction into confidence. The same can be said of the characters who appear in 'Romeo and Juliet', where Shakespeare meets *Sharp Objects*. This novella has been rearranged into three parts to best fit into a book of short fiction. Truths so intense they burn the eye.

Afterword

In recent months, I sat down with Rudrakshi's mother, who shared many memories of her, let me read her notebooks and journals, and permitted me to get a glimpse of the writer's life. Below are some episodes that stood out.

—·—

March 2008

Cats, birds, dogs and beetles vie for attention. At Yashbans Kennels, six-year-old R skips about, occasionally looking back at her mother who is still in the car.

Sammy, she yells suddenly, plucking a pup off its paws.

Sammy? Her mother peeps cautiously from the car.

Mommy, she shouts, come and meet Sammy, he is our dog.

Put him down, says her mother, not really a dog person herself.

Yashodhara, the farm in-charge, laughs and says, I think you own a dog now.

I don't know anything about dogs, R's mother says uncertainly.

You raised a child. This is easier. You can do it, Yashodhara assures her.

Sammy sits between R and her mother in the backseat. Bow-bow, says R and the dog grins back.

Back home, as her mother talks sternly to the dog (Sammy, sit! Sammy, get off my lap!), R is all smiles. She tells her father, Mommy is teaching Sammy English.

Afterword

December 2009

How much longer? asks R's younger cousin for the umpteenth time.

I told you, every time you ask we get late by that much more, replies R.

The girl falls quiet, but soon forgets and asks again, how much longer, how much longer.

On their way to Pondicherry, the girls are with their mothers. R's cousin is visiting from Delhi during school vacation and follows her around, saying proudly, I am your tail.

Which place is this? asks R's aunt.

Arni, says the driver.

Hmmm, go the mothers, looking out on to the endless hot roads. Suddenly a group of men and women dressed in bright, glittery clothes bursts out of nowhere on … bicycles! The mothers can't help but laugh; it seems to them a ridiculous sight, even surreal.

R's face falls. She says, Why are you making fun of the people of Arni? This place belongs to them. We are the intruders.

June 2010

In London, on a holiday with her family, R stops to stare at the poster for a play. *The 39 Steps*. The manager of the theatre shakes his head; children, alas, not allowed. 'Come back in a few years, dearie, we will still be running it!' he says in his British accent.

Disappointed by her own youth, R turns her attention to the sun-dappled graveyard they just passed. Could she linger there, please, please?

Her mother protests as she finds the idea morbid, but R insists.

R's parents exchange a resigned look. Her mother waves father and daughter off, Go do your thing. You are the nature lovers! I will sit here and wait for you.

———•———

In the seaside town of Ryde on the Isle of Wight, R stands with hands on hips, her thin cotton dress billowing, enjoying the breeze with eyes closed. She loves the rocks and the cliffs, the small butterflies and the big breakfasts, has half a mind to plead with her parents that they move here permanently…

A gang of bikers on their Harley Davidsons revs up the road. R's mother moves closer to her, in protective mommy mode. As the bikers zoom past, R runs after them, waving. 'How wonderful to ride away and feel the wind in your face,' she says to her mother.

February 2013

Her vocabulary is too advanced, her English teacher tells her mother at PTM, and her mother tries not to look proud. That's a good thing, isn't it? she asks on the way back from school.

Later in 2013

Bougainvillea wraps the pillars in the courtyard in papery pinks and whites at the Peacock Hotel — R's name for a resort in Madurai. The peacocks are in a flamboyant mood. They mince across the grass as if waiting for their dance teacher to arrive. Breadcrumbs in hand, R approaches a peacock *because this one has a philosopher's air*. The peacock bites her hand.

It bites? Peacock is so beautiful and it bites? Let down terribly, R revises her entire theory of aesthetics in an instant.

A bird once bit her finger and as fast as a river she bled. She had no time to linger, for her end was fast ahead. She ran from king to beggar searching for a cure, but not one soul could help her for her life was already torn. But she never gave up her search, she travelled on and on, never stopping to quench her thirst she travelled all the way to dawn, until her knees crumbled and forward she fell. With her last breath, she mumbled, 'Pretty bird, I will kill you as well!'

2014

R spreads out newly bought novels on a table, her eyes shiny with reader-ecstasy. A book just read, a book yet to be read…

How much you read, her mother grumbles. Every weekend they go to second-hand bookstores and haul back bags and bags of books. All her friends are always complaining that their kids don't read. She says, How I envy them!

R grins and says, Be careful what you wish for.

And how much you write! her mother continues to mock-grumble. She herself had designed a special writing desk, a sturdy thing with four legs and multiple drawers, so that R could sit and plot, chew her pen, type away at odd hours to her heart's content.

Can you, asks R hesitantly, leave me in a café on the way back, like, alone?

Her mother raises an eyebrow.

So I can write.

By the time her mother comes to pick her up from the café, after having sat in the car waiting for her just a little distance away, to give her the feeling of solitude that she so craved, R has scribbled away for a good two hours.

August 2014

In her diary, Rudrakshi writes —

In that place I've never been, nor have I seen, no one lives alone, no one dies lonely. Everyone lives in peace. In this place I've never been, over there animals have the freedom to talk, over there no one is mocked, no one is judged or scorned, there is no reason to mourn. This place thrives on dreams, hope, wishes. I really miss this place I've never been.

July 2015

Under a beach umbrella in Santa Monica, R stretches her legs till she is in danger of slipping off. The piers, the sunshine, each wave grunting as it crashes, the frizz in her hair … I can stay here forever, she declares.

Is it the sunset, asks her mother, or the blue of the water?

Just a million people talking about a million things around me.

———•———

Typewriter? echoes R's mother dubiously. You want a typewriter? You have an iPhone and a fancy computer.

But R stands motionless before the typewriter in a museum in Los Angeles.

She says she has the odd feeling of having used one before, in a previous lifetime perhaps, of tearing up papers and throwing them into corners for not reading her heart, her mind, for staying stubbornly blank.

Mother and daughter look at the typewriter, which looks back with no particular expression.

If you put paper in it, it will talk, says R.

Sometime in 2016

What is this story you've written? scolds R's mother. It is too dark. You know you like swimming, but this sounds like you hate it, like you are being forced to swim.

This is why I don't show you anything I write! I am a writer; I take a trigger from real life and make up the rest. This is the story of some other girl somewhere. Not mine.

But people will say … her mother tries to explain.

Then they don't understand fiction. Fiction is not the writer's own life story, that's autobiography. I wrote 'La Mer' because it occurred to me as something that could have happened to someone somewhere.

Look at your final portfolio submission for the Stanford class. Don't get me wrong, I am amazed. But also taken aback. What can a fourteen-year-old know of heartbreak, of the grief of a mother losing a child?

R looks mildly disgusted and says, See, that's why my creative-writing professor said don't show everything you write to your mother.

R's mother swallows hard. I will read as a friend, not a mother.

I'm a writer when I write, not a daughter.

July 2016

Rudrakshi's story 'A Vacancy' was the best story written in our class, and was in fact better than most undergraduate stories I have read. I don't think I was able to fully express to Rudrakshi how impressive it was in class, and so I am glad to have a second chance to do so now. I know Rudrakshi has many academic interests and demands, but I hope she continues to make time for her writing – she has great talent: a gift for voice, a proclivity for language, and a willingness to embrace strangeness, darkness and nuance in her art. Her story skirted unearned sentiment and melodrama and embedded us in the heart and mind of a narrator in the midst of trauma. This ability is quite rare in a young writer.

Excerpted from Ben Hoffman's evaluation certificate for Rudrakshi. Hoffman was her instructor at the creative writing workshop she attended at Stanford University.

2017

Offered conditional admission at an Ivy League college on the strength of her writing, R appears to be in a daze and follows her mother down the flowery path outside the university after the interview.

She stops suddenly, her mother stumbles into her from behind.

I know, says her mother, because she does. This is big and unexpected, an honour. Later she will call up her husband to share the good news, but right now the two of them need to soak it in like the sunshine and the smell of sweet pea around them. This 'little tall' girl of hers could be going away from home soon, for too long. R's mother looks around at the grey buildings, the hostel quarters nearby.

Can you, asks her mother carefully, see yourself here?

She is herself grappling with a sudden sense of future loss, of unanswered phone calls and emails, of the silence that will mean new friends, a new life for her only child. Why do children grow up and leave?

Afterword

Then she thinks back to the just-concluded interview when R spoke of her favourite books to Jamie-Lee Josselyn, the director of the Summer Workshop for Young Writers at the Kelly Writers House, University of Pennsylvania. How animated she had been. How full of things to say. R's mother had felt happily excluded, sitting back to watch someone in black-and-white go fully colour. That's the chirpiest she'd ever seen R.

———•———

Let's take a picture on the steps, R's mother says. It's their week in New York; R loves the Met (Metropolitan Museum of Art). An old man is sketching on the steps, two bananas in a brown paper bag beside him.

R says, Mama, I think that's all his lunch is. Let's buy his sketches, that will give him some more lunch money. Also, more people may stop by, seeing us buy. He will get more customers.

At their home, these still hang in the living room, reminders of a faraway, warm afternoon.

———•———

Rudrakshi's father remembers the long walks and longer talks they had every night.

She'd say she likes that I don't tell her that the stars are twinkling. That to me, like to her, stars are just a scientific phenomenon. He adds almost apologetically, I am not an advisor kind of dad ... This was just an hour to watch things side by side.

She got her unsentimental nature from him, she used to say. He doesn't care about offending others or making a listener feel bad; to him an argument is a complete act in itself, with a beginning, middle and end. It has to conclude logically. This reassured her somewhat.

He recalls how she would scowl when he sometimes said, I have to read up to talk to you! Your questions are too much for me!

Funny Daddy, she chided, to think she will ever know more than him one day.

Will she be so grown-up ever that she will consider herself done with knowing?

————•————

Since her return from Johns Hopkins University, Maryland, where she attended the Engineering Innovation residential course in July 2017, R has been feeling this sense of urgency to … She tries to describe it to her mother. At first she isn't sure what it is, but it is there always with her, this breathless feeling that something has to be done *just now* and she is maybe already late for it.

Connecting with the e-Vidyaloka organization, downloading Skype for the first time calms her somewhat, makes her feel she is on the right path; then an interview with them and an on-boarding session. She begins to take classes, teaching class seven in a remote village in Jharkhand. Initially shocked at how much they lagged behind and obsessed with ways to better their learning methods, she talks earnestly to the household help, who is originally from Jharkhand and has become an integral part of their family, to understand the difficulties of village life and the dismal educational facilities available to them.

Over the next three months, she has to think on her feet. She realizes quickly that she has to be innovative with the syllabus. By accident she discovers that the children love 'Johny Johny Yes Papa' the nursery rhyme, so this is what she pegs most of her lessons on. She teaches nouns and verbs set to 'Johny Johny', and all the forty kids assigned to her learn as fast as they can.

Thank god for Johny and his sweet tooth.

———•———

R runs a finger along the books on the shelf, her allies. Virginia Woolf, Sylvia Plath, Edith Wharton … Dante's *Inferno*, Aristotle's *The Art of Rhetoric*, David Foster Wallace's *Infinite Jest*, J.D. Salinger's *Catcher in the Rye*, Vladimir Nabokov's *Lolita*, Ernest Hemingway's *The Old Man and the Sea,* William Faulkner's *The Sound and the Fury*, Elizabeth Jane Howard's *The Sea Change.* And Alexander Pushkin's *Love Poems.*

You have a favourite word, Mom?

Attraversiamo. It means 'let's cross over' in Italian. What about you? What's yours?

All words and no word.

———•———

P.S. Sheer gratitude to Jeet Thayil for early praise; to Jahnavi Barua for reading; to Udayan Mitra, Rahul Soni and Sohini

Basak at HarperCollins India for the instant 'yes'; and to Debasree Bhattacharjee and Ratnadip Bhattacharjee, parents who took on the task of locating the writings with what could have only been the heaviest of hearts.